UNDERCOVER HACKER

WHITE HAT SECURITY, BOOK 4

LINZI BAXTER

Undercover Hacker
White Hat Security Series, Book 4
Copyright © 2018 by Linzi Baxter
Kindle Edition
Editor: Jennifer Wadsworth, Red Adept Editing
Cover Artist: Cassy Roop, Pink Ink Designs

All rights reserved. Except for use in any review, the reproduction or utilization of this work, in whole or in part, in any form by any electronic, mechanical, or other means now known or hereafter invented, is forbidden without permission of the author.

The unauthorized reproduction or distribution of this copyrighted work is illegal. Criminal copyright infringement (including infringement without monetary gain) is investigated by the FBI and is punishable by up to five years in federal prison and a fine of $250,000.

Please purchase only authorized electronic editions, and do not participate in or encourage the electronic piracy of copyrighted materials. Your support of the author's rights is appreciated.

This is a work of fiction. Names, characters, businesses, places, events, and incidents are either the products of the author's imagination or used in a fictitious manner. Any resemblance to actual persons, living or dead, or actual events is purely coincidental.

BLURB

A woman set on revenge

Sophie has spent the last twenty years looking for her sister and the people who killed her parents. She works undercover for a man she loathes because he's promised her information and assistance in her search. Though she's determined not to be distracted from her quest for family and revenge, she nonetheless finds herself drawn to Agent White, a CIA agent who may be looking for the same people. No matter how tempting Agent White's handcuffs are, she will not let a man come between her and her goal.

A spy who only works alone

Agent White's boss, the director of the CIA, sends him to arrest Sophie Stewart without giving him any further details. He doesn't expect to come face to face with the most beautiful and fiery woman he has ever seen. A loner by preference, he's never wanted more than a one-night stand with any woman. However, something about Sophie calls to his inner soul. With one look at Sophie, Agent White knows he wants something permanent with her.

The more Agent White learns about Sophie, the more he is determined to keep her safe and never let her go. But for him to do that, Sophie has to stop hiding her secrets – even if those secrets change the course of their lives. Will Agent White be able to save Sophie before time runs out?

DEDICATION

To all the amazing readers!

ACKNOWLEDGMENTS

I would like to express my gratitude to the many people who saw me through this book: My editor, Jennifer, who did an amazing job and worked hard to help me craft a better story. Cassy for doing an astounding job with the cover art. Michelle for taking the time to beta read for me. My husband and family for always being there to support me. This book couldn't have happened without all of you!

Thank you to all you amazing readers who are going on this journey alongside me. I hope *Undercover Hacker* is all that you hoped for and more!

AUTHOR'S NOTE

White Hat Security Series

Hacker Exposed

Royal Hacker

Misunderstood Hacker

Undercover Hacker

Hacker Revelation 7/31/2018

The Steele Brothers Series

Montana Fortune 6/26/2018

Visit linzibaxter.com for more information and release dates.
Join Linzi Baxter Newsletter at Newsletter

PROLOGUE - SOPHIE

Sophie – Twenty-five years ago

"Soph, I'm scared."

A loud gunshot reverberated through the house. At the sound of my mother's scream, Kat launched herself into bed next to me.

Kat had tears streaming down her face at the sound of our mother's blood-curdling scream. She cried harder, not understanding that we needed to be quiet. Someone was in the house, and I needed to protect Kat.

"Maaamaaa!"

I put my finger to my lips, motioning that we needed to be silent. Her little headed bobbed, showing me she understood. I tiptoed over to the door and listened for voices or footsteps. I reached for the doorknob and flipped the lock, hoping to keep out whoever had come into our house in the middle of the night.

It had to be robbers. I could hear shouting downstairs, and it wasn't voices I recognized. When a gun fired and I heard the scream from my mom, I knew these were evil people.

After getting the door locked, I tiptoed back to the bed and motioned for Kat to follow me. She was still sniffling from crying. I reached for her hand and pulled her over to the closet. Shoes and stuffed animals lined the floor. Kat sat on the floor next to me, and we gradually closed the two slatted closet doors. We worked to arrange the stuffed animals on top of us, trying to hide in plain sight.

"Soph, I want Mommy."

"I know, Kat, but we need to stay here until we hear Mom's voice. There are bad people out there."

"Why are bad people in our house?" She had her thumb stuck in her mouth, which caused the words to come out muffled.

When I heard loud footsteps coming down the hall, I reached over and pulled Kat to my side. It was my job to protect her. The doorknob jiggled a couple of times, and muffled sounds came from the other side of the door. When the grumbling stopped, I held my breath, hoping the footsteps would continue down the hall. Instead, I heard a loud thud followed by the sound of the wood door cracking.

It was so dark in the closet that I couldn't see Kat's face. I hoped she could tell I had my finger up to my lips, warning her not to make a sound, lest she let the men know where we were.

"Where're the damn kids? He'll kill us both if we don't find them. That guy is a crazy mother fucker. I can't believe he took Tommy out for asking a simple question." The voice outside the door sounded wheezy.

"Yeah. I didn't wanna take this job, but once it's done, our slate's clean. The sooner we find these little brats, the sooner we can get gone."

From between the slats in the closet door, I could see two figures moving around in our room. The larger of the two men reached down and flipped my twin bed over. The loud crashing of the furniture made Kat and I jump, causing the closet floor to creak. I held my breath and pulled Kat closer, hoping we hadn't given away our location. It was hard to make out their faces or anything about them, but based on their conversation, they were the evil men.

We heard the thud of the men's footsteps as they approached the closet. Kat shook in my arms. She was merely five and had no understanding what these thugs were capable of. Being six years older than Kat, I had better understanding.

The door to the closet swung open with so much force that it dislodged from its tracks. Two men holding guns stood in front of us. Kat screamed in fear. The guy closest to her had bloodshed in his eyes. A large hand reached into the closet and grabbed Kat. He was able to pull her with so much force that I couldn't hang on. A smaller man reached down to grab me. I kicked my legs out, hoping to send the man off-balance. It only caused him to get angry. I didn't see his hand coming until it was too late. He hit me across the side of the face with enough force to send my head flying back to crash into the wall.

Before I had a chance to reevaluate the situation, the bigger man grabbed me. When he pressed me against his body, the smell of him made me gag. It was a mixture of body odor and alcohol.

"Let's take them downstairs," the smaller, nasally-voiced fellow hollered at the big man. Both men had long, greasy hair and wore motorcycle vests with matching symbols—a skull with angel wings and the words "The Reapers" underneath the symbol.

Needing to get free, I shifted in the man's grasp and bit his tattooed arm as hard as I could. He had the same symbol from his vest tattooed on his arm. I vowed I would find this man one day and end him and his gang. He grunted at the pain of the bite. Then I was flying through the air, and my head knocked against the door jamb.

"Dumb bitch! Why'dya you do that? I'll teach you what happens when you bite someone."

Each word he screamed at me was followed by a kick. I could feel my ribs crack.

"Dude, stop! That guy downstairs will end you if you kill her. That fucker is scary as shit, and he wants these kids for some damn reason."

The overgrown thug gave me one last kick that knocked the breath out of me. The world had gone blurry from the tears running down my face. He grabbed me by the hand and dragged me to the living room, not caring if I hit things along the way. The closer we got to the living room, the louder my mom's sobs became. She was pleading with someone to leave. Mom said she would do everything they asked if they would just let her children go.

"What took you so long? I've had to keep this whiney bitch alive to make sure you found the kids."

Two more men stood in the living room. My father was on the couch, body leaning forward. I could see blood seeping from his chest. One of the men stood in the shadows next to my father, his gun pointed at my mom. The second man was keeping watch out the window. The living room lights were off. The sole light in the room came from the street lamps shining in through the window, so I couldn't see their faces.

"Please. I will sign everything over to you. You don't have to do this," my mom pleaded. She was on the couch next to Dad with her arms tied together in front of her. Tears streamed down her checks, and a bruise bloomed on her face where someone must have hit her.

The ogre who had dragged me into the living room dropped me on the floor near my mom. He must have assumed I wouldn't try anything else after my beating. He was wrong. No matter what, I would always try to save my family.

The man in the shadows glanced in my direction then pointed at me. "Is there a reason she looks like you beat the crap out of her?" He sounded angry. It was hard to tell, though, because he was talking through something that made it hard to hear.

"She gave me problems."

The man pointed his gun at the thug who had dragged me from my room and pulled the trigger. The sound of the gun echoed through the living room. Then he pointed to the other thug.

"Hurry up and kill the bitch. Grab the children, and let's move."

The man in the shadows had done me a favor. That was one less person I would need to find and kill.

From his calm demeanor and the way the men looked nervous around him, I knew he was the leader and one of the men I would come after. If I made it out of this situation alive, my life's mission would be to identify this man and kill him.

The nasally man, who had dragged Kat from the bedroom and shoved her onto the couch, pointed his gun at my mom. His hand was shaking, as though he was scared for his life. His friend lay on the floor, not moving.

My mom was the sweetest woman in the world and would never hurt a fly. How could these men want her dead? Kat was on the couch next to my mom. I was on the floor, only a few feet away. They thought I had passed out.

"Nooo!"

I launched myself in front of the gun at the same time it went off. The bullet hit me in the stomach. Pain radiated through me so strongly that the world went black. The last thing I remember is two more guns shots.

I COULD HEAR the muttering of people around me and a faint beeping in the background. My limbs felt heavy. I reflected on the last thing I could recall—the memory of the men who had invaded my house. The last thing I remembered was jumping in front of the bullet. I wondered if my mom and Kat were okay. If I had made it, maybe they had, too, and were in the room with me. I listened hard to the voices.

"Did they find the men responsible for hurting this child? I want to take them to a dark alley and teach them a lesson."

"No. I hate when we see cases like this come in. They're always the hardest."

Then silence again. I couldn't open my eyes, and I was so tired that I fell back to sleep, hoping the next time I came awake, my mom's voice would be the one I heard.

"Oh, the poor girl. Did you find who did this?"

"No. I don't think the police will find the people responsible. This girl is special. I want to do this outside of child protective services. I will send you money every month until she graduates, and when I want to see her, I will." The voice sounded familiar, but I couldn't open my eyes to see who it was. They were still so heavy.

"Oh, we have always wanted children, but don't have enough money for an adoption. Of course we'll take her, Juan. You can see her whenever you want for giving us this gift. Did the authorities find her sister?"

I don't want to live with this woman. I want my

mom. Why is my mom not in the room? Kat's missing? Why won't my lips move so I can ask questions?

"I will pay for the therapy she'll need to deal with losing her parents and her sister. The doctor told me she had to have a salpingectomy. While the doctor was able to save one of her Fallopian tubes, Sophie has a very slim chance of ever having children."

I had lost my mom and my dad. Having kids was the furthest thing from my mind. From this point forward, my sole objective in life would be to find my sister and eliminate the men who had destroyed my family. I remembered what the tattoo looked like, so I would start with him. No matter what happened in the future, my only goal would be to get Kat back. Kat was the only family I had left.

1

SOPHIE

The stress of living a double life was wearing on me. Withholding information from Bridget was making my stomach turn. I knew that if I told my longtime friend and boss what had happened in the past and what I was doing now, she would help. Not wanting to drag my friends into my dark past, I made a deal with the devil to get me closer to my goal. But, the devil kept requesting more of me without giving me the information I needed to take down the people who killed my family.

The devil would figure out soon that I had hacked their system to get the information about Jessica's kidnappers. When the trail led back to my computer, they would come for me this time. They had been waiting for an excuse to bring me in and make me work for them full time. Jessica was worth what I would go through.

Jessica had been kidnapped by a terrorist organization. She had become part of my family. Her twin sister used to work for us at White Hat Security before she met Sam, her fiancé. Now Patty and Sam were living in Shialia, working to take over the crown.

Jessica's fiancé, Brock, was a skilled hacker, but he didn't have access to the same files I did. Jessica and Patty's dad was the king of Shialia, and he had slept around. Axmed had been the king's illegitimate son and the head of the terrorist organization that went after Jessica ten years ago. They had gone after her again recently. After she had been kidnapped, I hacked into a database to discover the details needed to get her back. Brock and his group rescued Jessica before she was killed.

The shouting from the reception area of White Hat Security brought me back to the present. Bridget's voice went from yelling to screaming. A loud *bang* had me moving faster. I figured I had better go calm her down before I had to bail her out jail.

"Miss, we are here for Sophie Stewart. This has nothing to do with you."

The sound of my full name had me slowing my steps. I peered around the corner to see a few men in black suits. I knew they were here for me. Needing to hide a couple of things before they took me in, I hightailed it back to my office. Bridget would hold them off. She was either trying to protect me or to give me time to hide what I needed to before these men got to me. The pink external drive plugged into the front of my computer contained the work I did for the devil. I removed the drive and hid it in the ceiling tiles. I grabbed my purse and headed back to the reception area.

"I don't care who you think you are. I want to see a warrant. You can't just come in here and demand to talk to my employees without some form of documentation. We do nothing illegal here." Bridget was screaming. The whole office stood around her, trying to figure out what was going on.

A man stood in front of Bridget with his arms crossed. The black tailored suit fit him perfectly. He was tall, close to six foot five. His hair was dark brown, and his brown eyes looked tormented from years of working for the devil. He was close to losing his temper. He kept pinching the bridge of his nose, trying to stay calm. At least if I was being arrested, it would be by this man. He was hot. Like, panty-dropping hot.

The sexy man pinched his nose one more time before saying, "Ma'am, tell me where Sophie Stewart is before I take you into custody for obstructing justice."

Bridget walked toward the tall drink of water. Her

pink high heels gave her a minor height boost, but the man Bridget was about to go toe-to-toe with still towered over her. I knew I needed to step in before she ended up in federal custody. She had no clue who she was dealing with. I, on the other hand, knew precisely what was going on.

I walked out from around the corner. The sexy man in the form-fitting black suit looked up to see me. He headed around Lacey's reception desk toward me, moving with an athletic grace that seemed effortless. If he hadn't been wearing the standard-issue spy getup, I still would've known he was special ops by the way he moved. Bridget went after him. Before she ended up in more trouble, I needed to get this under control.

"Bridget, it's okay."

"Say nothing. I have Alex coming down with Antonio."

The man, who I assumed was in charge, continued making his way toward me. He was the only one that had been talking to Bridget. The other agents just stared. Bridget made many people speechless. He cleared his throat before saying, "Sophie Stewart, I'm Agent White. Will you please come with us, or do we need to handcuff you?"

I couldn't resist playing with him. "Well, Agent White, I know that's not your real name. You need to stop with the color coding. If you're putting the handcuffs on, I would prefer the pink fuzzy ones. I like the kinky side of things."

Agent White didn't have time to reply to my comment before Antonio and Alex walked in the front door. This was getting out of control. I needed to go with Agent White before someone ended up doing something they regretted.

Antonio walked over to where Agent White and I were standing. He looked pissed. "Agent White, do you want to explain why you are trying to take Sophie into custody?"

"Stay out of this, Antonio. This comes from the director. I need to take her in."

"Why was I not informed about this case?" The vein in Antonio's head was throbbing.

How does Antonio know Agent White, and why would he be informed about the devil's cases?

"This is not your concern. Stop asking questions."

The pissing contest needed to end. "Agent White, let's go so we can get this over with."

"Sophie, you don't know what you're saying. You don't know who these people are. If you go with them, we might not be able to get you out." Antonio spun and looked at Agent White. "You don't have jurisdiction on US soil."

Agent White's next words brought the dread to the forefront. "Sophie Stewart, you are under arrest for treason." He reached around to cuff my hands and pushed me out the door.

I could hear Bridget in the back, demanding Antonio do something. But there wasn't anything he could do to get me out of my situation. I only hoped it would get me closer to my sister.

I twisted to take one last look at my life. Bridget was in tears, and Alex had his arms wrapped around her. He looked like he wanted to kill someone for making his wife cry. Antonio was screaming into the phone, and the remaining staff seemed shocked or close to tears.

Agent White assisted me into the back seat of a black SUV. He walked around to the other side and sat next to me. I held my wrists out to him. "These are unnecessary."

"I think you are more dangerous than the director knows. But he would be mad if I hurt his pet." He reached over and unlocked the cuffs.

I didn't think the director would consider me his pet. We had been at each other's throats for years.

"Do you want to tell me where you're taking me or why you came for me?" I was planning on playing dumb until they showed me proof of what I did wrong. I wouldn't put it past this organization to pin a false accusation on me so that I had to work for them all the time, not just when I wanted.

Agent White shifted in his seat. From the look on his face, he was uncomfortable with this assignment. "You know what you did."

"Nope. Since you won't tell me what evidence you planted, do you want to tell me why Antonio knew your name? Well, your fake name."

The sexy man shook his head and looked forward. It seemed I wouldn't get any answers out of him. I spent the remaining car ride figuring out a plan to either escape or get out of the mess. One speck of hope was that Antonio knew where I might be going.

When I looked out the window, I noticed we were heading to an airstrip. My stomach took a nose dive at the sight of the strip. I had a feeling we were on our way to DC to see the devil himself. But, I was in for another surprise, since the devil was waiting for me on the plane.

"Sophie. It's so nice of you to join us," he barked.

Director Sanchez's voice could command a room. Everyone listened when he spoke. Well, almost everyone. I couldn't give a flying fuck what the man had to say. Twenty years ago, he made me a promise he still hasn't fulfilled.

He came to my adopted family's house on my sixteenth birthday, asking if I would train under his men and help him with undercover work. If I did, he would help find my sister or at least what happened to her. My foster parents were kind but lacked money. If I could help them by working with this man, I would. I thought maybe one day we could move out of the slums, and I would find my sister. It had been twenty-five years since she went missing, but I had hope she was still alive.

"Did I have an option? You know Antonio will come after me. Why didn't you just call me in?"

"You took that option away when you hacked our network. Antonio works for me. I'll get him to drop his bulldozing. And I tried calling you numerous times. You weren't answering."

"Is it hacking when I have access?" I asked. "Sucks when you want something and can't have it."

The devil took a sip of Scotch and pointed to the white leather seat next to him. "Those files are classified. And, I always get my way. You're here, aren't you?"

I shrugged. Not wanting to give him any satisfaction, I sat in the seat across from him. "What do you want?"

He let out a long sigh and closed his eyes at my outward disrespect. "It's time I tell you why I haven't let you find your sister."

This is the carrot he always dangled in front of me to keep me in line. I would help him with his cases. He would give me a little information about my sister. I had looked for the files they had on her. They weren't on any of the servers. I had a feeling the director kept them in a safe so I couldn't reach them.

"Is this where you give me a little information so I fall back in line," I said with disgust in my voice.

"No. This is where I tell you that, if you want to see your sister, you will become a full-time agent and work with Agent White. The case you will be given will lead you to your sister. Do you agree to come work for me for the next ten years?"

If it led to my sister, I would do anything. Agent White was sitting in the chair across from us, watching the exchange. It wouldn't exactly be a hardship to work with that man.

"Kat and I have been apart for twenty-five years. I've worked for you the past twenty. Have you known where she was this entire time and kept her from me? If I don't find her in the next six months, you have no deal."

"You'll find her by then."

"Then yes, I will take the job."

An evil grin spread across his face. "Welcome to the CIA, Agent Red."

2

ZANE

I watched Sophie look at Director Sanchez with anger in her eyes. The director was a lean man. He was dressed in a perfectly-ironed black Armani suit and a crisp white shirt. He had one leg crossed over his knee, showing off his new Italian leather shoes. It was obvious that if Sophie didn't need something from him, she would take him out. There was pure hatred in her eyes.

Director Sanchez always got what he wanted, because he had something over the person he needed a favor from. However, Director Sanchez had nothing on me. I just worked for him. Lately, I'd noticed that he was losing control, and I thought bringing Sophie in was his way of trying to fix one of his mistakes. I would call my brother later today to let him know the CIA

Director was up to something. I had a feeling it wasn't something good.

I didn't trust the man. I should've asked more questions about taking Sophie in. After my last operation, I had needed something easy, and bringing in one woman had seemed easy. Now, I was second guessing that thought.

"No. This is where I tell you that, if you want to see your sister, you will become a full-time agent and work with Agent White," Sanchez explained. At the sound of my code name, I tuned in more closely to the conversation. In the ten years I had worked for the CIA, I very seldom had a partner. I wondered if my brother was plotting something. I needed to talk to the man more often.

Brad, another agent who was sitting next to me, snorted. He understood that I didn't work well with others. This mission had been thrown at me this morning. The director had told me to bring Sophie in. I wasn't given any case notes on the op, but they said she knew why she was being taken in. Being around Sophie for the last hour made me realize she was more dangerous than anyone knew.

"When do we start working on the assignment?" Sophie asked.

Director Sanchez leaned back and took another sip

of his Scotch. "We'll head to Langley once we land and get you and Agent White up to speed."

Sophie tilted her head toward me. "You don't know what our assignment is?" Since getting on the plane, this was the first time Sophie had acknowledged me. I, on the other hand, had a difficult time peeling my eyes away from her body.

The white leather seat squeaked under me as I leaned forward. "The only thing I was told this morning was to bring you in. I had no idea I was getting a partner." Hiding the annoyance in my voice was hard. Director Sanchez had had plenty of time to tell me his plans.

Sophie turned back to Director Sanchez and kept talking. It gave me time to study her. She was stunning. Her fiery red hair was up in a messy bun. The freckles on her nose proved she was a natural redhead. She had the prettiest deep-green eyes. Her lips were plump, and all I could think about was having those lips wrapped around my cock.

Fuck. Just looking at her sent my body out of control. All of a sudden, my pants became uncomfortable.

The jerk of the plane hitting the tarmac brought me out of my lust-induced thoughts.

SIX CIA ANALYSTS sat in the war room at Langley. I grabbed a seat at the front of the room next to the director. Sophie slid into the place next to me. She was shifting in her chair, looking uncomfortable. Before I had time to ask her why, the director started the session.

An image of a man in his late sixties appeared on the projection screen. The gasp next to me had me turning in Sophie's directing. The color had drained from her face.

"You mother fucker!" Sophie launched from her seat. "You told me he was dead. You said, and I quote, 'The whole Reapers motorcycle gang is dead, including the president.' That man does not look dead." At Sophie declaration, everyone's attention had swung from the screen to her.

Director Sanchez sighed and sat back in his chair. "You need to keep your temper under control, Red. Our goal is to take down his network. I didn't need you getting yourself killed when you were a kid. I told you that, when you were old enough, you could go after the individuals that hurt your family. The Reapers have become worthless, and the agency no longer needs them. Who will lead us to your target? Your specialization is hacking, not assassination."

Sophie mumbled something inaudible under her breath.

"This photo was taken two days ago in, Moscow." Steve, the senior analyst, went on to explain the intel the agency had received. Steve was small for a man. His brown hair was messy and unkempt. He was the best analyst the CIA had. Sophie and I were lucky to have Steve working on our side. "We think Yermushin is selling something to Russia."

Sophie leaned forward, resting her elbows on the table. "What is Yermushin selling?" Sophie's voice was raw with emotion.

I already knew what Yermushin was selling. Earlier, the director had said the agency no longer needed him and we could take him down. But the CIA had been trying to take Yermushin into custody for ages. He seemed to slip through our grasp each time. The director's words contradicted everything I thought I knew. I had been after Yermushin for years. The CIA had a plant in his organization, but the plant couldn't reveal much without blowing her cover. She would give us tips but never enough to bring him down.

"He's selling women on the black market. Do we have a date for the next auction?" Director Sanchez asked, his face neutral, not giving any sign of what he was thinking.

Steve reached for the envelope in front of him. He flipped through a couple of pages before responding.

"It's scheduled for next week. We believe it will take place at a fundraiser in New York."

Before anyone had time to respond, the conference room door swung open. The bright light from the hallway blinded me, so I couldn't see who stood in the doorway. I could only see two massive shadows.

"Someone forgot to send my party invite," the more massive silhouette stated matter-of-factly.

Antonio Ross. I would recognize his voice anywhere. It held a hint of a threat. He wasn't a man of many words, and when he spoke, people either listened or disappeared. He might be out of the military, but the POTUS and the CIA called on him and his company often to fill contracts.

Not waiting for an invitation, Antonio and the person with him headed toward the seats on the other side of Sophie. With a motion of his hand, Antonio waved the two analysts from the chairs. I didn't recognize his companion. He was tall, blond, and built like a football player. He sat next to Sophie, and I heard him ask whether she was okay. It sounded like genuine concern in his voice.

"I told you to stay out of this." Director Sanchez rose from his chair and leaned forward on the conference table to get his point across.

Antonio leaned back in the chair he had commandeered from the analyst. "See, that's where you've always been wrong, Director." Antonio's voice dripped with hatred. "I don't take orders from you. My orders come from someone a lot higher than you." Antonio's gaze never wavered from the director's. "Are you saying I need to make that call to be in this meeting? You took someone from my family without cause."

Sophie went to speak, but the man sitting next to her grabbed her hand and shook his head. The gesture made me want to rip the guy's arm off.

Director Sanchez had a smirk on his face, as if he were about to win a game. "Sophie agreed to work here. This is her and Agent White's case. I will have you removed from this building if you don't leave."

Antonio was known for being one of the best of the hired mercenaries the government used on contract. He was called on by top officials all the time. If the director didn't want him on this case, it meant he was up to something. There was no way I would let Sophie come to harm. I had only met her this morning, but something deep inside me wanted to protect her from the surrounding people. I had a trump card I could pull on the director. In all the years I had worked for him, I had never used it.

"I don't mind him working the case with us. If Antonio wants to volunteer, who am I to complain?"

"No!" the director screamed. He reached for the conference room phone and dialed security. Before he hit the last button, I reached over and clicked the line off. I could handle having the director on my bad side. But, Antonio and I went way back, and I didn't want to make an enemy of him.

It took a second for the director to get his bearings. "Agent White, I will ruin your career."

I had never taken kindly to being threatened. Most men who had threatened me were six feet under. However, this conference room wasn't the best place in which to kill the director.

I knew the grunt of laughter to my left came from Antonio. He was the one person in the room who had seen me lose my shit before. Needing to get my temper under control, I took a few calming breaths. "Sit down, Director." I pointed to his chair. "Here is how this will go down. Antonio and his friend will help Sophie and me on this case. Then you will give her the information she needs without her having to work for you for ten more years." I could hear the anger in my voice. He had played with her life for too many years.

"You can't speak to me like that."

"Everyone out." When the room didn't clear, I said, "Now!" The analysts scurried out the exit, running each other over. Steve got up to leave with the rest of them, but I caught his eye and pointed to his chair, indicating he should stay.

"Director, I think you forget who I am. I'm an agent

because it's what I like to do. I could have your job with one call, so don't push me. Antonio could get the same result with a call. The difference is that I've never made that call before, so I'm sure my brother will do what I ask."

The blood drained from the director's face as he remembered who I was. People were so used to working with me that they forgot who I was related to. "You would really drag Zack into this?"

I knew I had him where I wanted him. "Yes, and it's President Tucker to you."

"All right, you can use them. But I want to be kept informed about everything at all times!"

"With that out of the way, Agent White, this is Brock McKenzie. He owns Blackwood Security. Steve, please hand him a laptop," Antonio demanded. When it looked as though the director would protest, Antonio continued. "I'm letting you stay in this room as a courtesy. Steve could get me up to speed without you. If you want to stay, sit and shut up."

Sophie stood and paced. "Antonio, you don't know what's going on. I need Director Sanchez on my side. He can help me find my sister."

Antonio leveled a glare at Sophie. "Sit. If you had told us your sister was missing, you would have had her back by now. At the moment, I want to take you over my knee and redden your ass."

I couldn't hold back the anger that coursed through me at the thought of Antonio laying a hand on Sophie. "You can touch her over my dead body." I reached out, grabbed Sophie's arm, and brought her close to my side. I had never acted like this before, and I had no clue where the emotion was coming from.

The conference room went silent.

Antonio studied me for a long moment. "Fine. I will kill you if you hurt her."

After another moment, Brock broke the tension. "Since the pissing match is over, can we start on the case? I have a fiancé to get home to, and you are cutting into my time. So, let's go."

I took over the meeting. "We are going after Yermushin." I ignored the grunt that came from Antonio. He knew who the man was. "He is setting up a sale at a charity fundraiser in two weeks. Agent Red and I are working undercover at the fundraiser. Our goal is to figure out when the sale is going to take place. This is the first positive lead we have had on the man in ages."

"I'm going to kill him," Sophie mumbled.

Antonio's gaze locked on Sophie. He must have heard her. "Why are you going to kill him? How long have you been running cases for the director?"

The director took a breath to speak, but Antonio shook his head in warning.

Sophie pointed to the screen showing Yermushin's face. "That man and his gang dragged my sister and me out of our bedrooms when we were just kids, killed my parents in front of us, and kidnapped my sister."

Sophie took a deep breath. She was shaking. "Director Sanchez has been helping me try to find my sister for the past twenty years. Every so often he would dangle some fruit in front of me, but never enough to find her. Ten years ago, he told me he found the gang based off of the tattoo information I supplied and that Yermushin's gang had been killed off."

I cringed inwardly. The director had found someone who was good at computers, and he had used her. If her sister was still alive, he could have gotten her back years ago. He probably knew where she was and whether she was alive or dead. From the look on Antonio's face, he was thinking along the same lines.

"Steve, who is the contact that sent you the information? I need to do some checking so Sophie and I don't go in blind. We'll work the case from my safe house and connect into you directly for information."

Steve walked around the room, handing everyone a case file. "Everything is in the folder. The contact's name is Ice. Her photo is on page—"

"Give me those files," the director demanded. He scrambled from his seat, trying to get to us.

"No. No. No. She works for you? You were

stringing me along all these years? You didn't think I would recognize my sister?"

Sophie leaped from her chair and went after the director, her arm pulled back to punch him. I grabbed Sophie around the waist before she had time to assault the Director of the CIA.

"Let me go!" Sophie kicked her foot back, trying to take me out. When I didn't let up, she continued screaming. "You bastard! You've known where she's been? Let me go, fuck face. I'm going to kill him!"

Brock was standing between the director and us. Antonio's eyes never left the photograph in the file.

"I instructed you to remove those photos," the director yelled at Steve.

Knowing all I needed, I threw Sophie over my shoulder.

"We will take the case from here. It seems we can't trust you."

"I will have you wiped off the Earth for this," Director Sanchez rasped.

I heard heavy steps behind me. Brock and Antonio were on my heels.

SOPHIE

I'm not sure what was more shocking—finally

seeing a picture of my sister after these years or being manhandled by a sex god. "We need to go back. We need more information, and he might have you sent away."

Antonio and Brock both grunted with laughter. I raised my head just enough to glare at them both. They were supposed to be my friends. "I can't believe you two are letting Zane walk out. Did either of you hear what the director threatened? I'm not a child. Put me down. I need to find my sister!"

Antonio's eyes changed at the mention of my sister. It looked like a mixture of hurt and betrayal, which I didn't understand.

The loud smack echoed through the room, before I had time to register that the ogre of a man had smacked my ass. A second later, the pain registered with a fiery heat.

"We will get your sister and the man that killed your parents. We don't need the director. He can't harm me." Agent White laughed.

Once we made it to the parking lot, I was finally put on my feet. I couldn't hold in my emotions any longer, not sure if they were from being manhandled or from seeing the first picture of my sister in twenty-five years. I lunged at Agent White and punched his chest. He wrapped his arms around me and pulled me in.

"It's okay. We will find her. I promise," Agent

White whispered in my ear.

His hand running up and down my back settled me down. Feeling embarrassed, I stepped away from Agent White to wipe the tears from my face. Brock engulfed me in a hug that felt good. The loud crack of flesh hitting flesh had me jumping back to see what was going on.

"You knew my wife was alive?" Antonio growled. He lurched toward Agent White again.

Brock leaped forward and grabbed Antonio before he had time to throw a second punch.

"What are you talking about, man? I've never met your wife. You've never shown me a picture of her." The agent was standing up, wiping the blood dripping down his face with his sleeve.

Antonio pulled out the picture of my sister and pointed at her. "Zane, this is a picture of my dead wife, Kat."

"I swear I didn't know she was your wife. I've met her a couple times on assignment. Everyone says her husband is dead and she won't date."

This was getting too strange. "You're married to my sister?"

"I think we are uncovering too many secrets. Let's go to one of my safe houses and talk out a strategy. Not here, where cameras are watching us." Agent White pointed at the camera positioned on us.

3

ZANE

The tension in the car was so thick that it almost felt suffocating. Sophie had been quiet since we got in the SUV. I wanted to reach over, grab her hand, and let her know everything would be okay. The need to reassure her was eating at me. In the rearview mirror, I saw that Antonio had been staring at that photo for the past twenty minutes.

I had no alliance with the director. "Antonio, I swear, if I had known she was your wife, I would have told you. You've never shown me a picture of her or told me her name."

"I know you would have told me. I lost it back there. Let's get to the safe house and figure out what the director is after. It seems he's keeping things from us." Antonio shifted to stare out the window.

"Can you please explain why a stranger knows you're married and your family doesn't?" Brock looked annoyed that I had known something neither he nor Antonio's family knew.

A few years back, Antonio had asked if he could tag along on my op. He was led to believe the man we were going after had killed his wife. He wanted vengeance. The case was to eliminate the target. I gave Antonio the right to take the shot.

"We met on assignment. It was a whirlwind romance. We got married on the last day of our assignment. When we were having breakfast in a local cafe, a gun man started taking shots inside. I was hit. When I woke, the director told me she was dead and had no living rel—"

"Do I look like I'm fucking dead?" Sophie shifted in her seat to turn toward Antonio. "How could she do this? I've spent my life trying to find her and go after the men who killed our parents, and she fucking works for them. How can she look at that man every day knowing he killed our parents?"

"Let's work together and figure out what's going on. There must be more to the story than what we think. We're almost to the safe house."

I was taking Sophie to one of my many houses, one I kept in a shell company. Only one other person knew about it. The house was back in the mountains, and trees helped cover any satellite surveillance. It was hard not to notice the helicopter to the right of the house when we pulled up.

"Fuck." Things kept going wrong.

"He beat us here?" Antonio didn't need to look. He knew what my outburst was about.

At the same time, Sophie and Brock both asked, "Who?"

"My brother." I parked the car in the driveway, not storing it in the garage. "Leave your things in the car. When we are done talking to him, we'll need to head to another house."

Sophie opened her mouth, about to ask more questions. I shook my head. She would find out soon enough.

Antonio was halfway to the house before any of us got out of the car, probably going after my brother. I needed to step on it. My brother wouldn't be upset, but the people with him, would be.

"Fuck. Hurry! We need to stop Antonio," I yelled at Brock and Sophie.

I didn't look behind me. Sophie and Brock would come if they understood the urgency in my voice. I heard shouts coming from the kitchen area. I ran toward the noise and heard the clicking of Sophie's shoes behind me.

Antonio had my brother pressed up against the

wall, and three agents had guns pointed at him. Antonio wasn't paying attention to what the agents were doing. He had his sights on my brother.

I felt a tap on my shoulder.

"Um, Zane, the President of the United States is in your house."

"Older brothers are annoying like that, showing up univited."

"Oh."

Needing to get the situation back under control and keep Antonio from getting shot or killed, I said, "Antonio, stop killing my brother. Shouldn't you get your answers before taking out the person with the information? Also, you know how hard it is to get a clean-up crew out here?"

Antonio slowly removed his hands from my brother. When it looked like he would let go, he suddenly pulled his arm back and punched my brother in the side. Zack dropped to the floor, and the three agents jumped on top of Antonio.

Once Zack got his bearings, he demanded that the agents let Antonio go. Slowly, they released Antonio, waiting for him to attack again. The whole day had been a cluster fuck. I walked past my brother, who was leaning over and holding his side. Antonio was peeling himself off the floor. I reached into the fridge to grab a beer.

"Sophie, want a beer?" When I looked over my shoulder, her mouth was hanging open and she had a look of shock on her face. She nodded. I grabbed two beers and headed toward the living room. The posse of people would follow or kill each other.

"You aren't going to offer me a beer?" Zack asked.

"If you want one, grab it. I'm not your servant."

Sophie followed me to the living room. I heard grumbling from the kitchen and, a few seconds later, footsteps coming toward the living room. Sophie and I took a seat on the couch. I liked that she chose to sit next to me.

Zack, Brock, and Antonio showed up in the living room without the secret agents. Zack sat in the recliner next to the couch, sipping on a cold beer. Antonio paced back and forth in front of the big-screen TV. Brock grabbed his laptop and sat in the last chair in the room.

"You want to tell me why you compromised my safe house?" My voice was laced with anger. Zack could have called. Anywhere he went was traceable, and his being here would lead Director Sanchez right to us.

Zack leaned back in the chair, staring down at his beer before answering. "I got a call from Director San—"

"You mean the devil," Sophie seethed.

Zack let out a chuckle before continuing. "Okay, we have renamed my Director of the CIA, as the devil. This afternoon, I got a call from"—Zack held up his hands and made air quotes—"the devil, and he informed me that he was going after you and Antonio because you kidnapped his agent and threatened him. He also informed me that he has people that can confirm his story."

Sophie leaped off the couch before I could stop her. "That is not true. You can't take him in. They're my only hope at figuring out what happened to my sister. The devil has been manipulating me for ages."

I reached up, grabbed Sophie, and dragged her into my lap. Zack gave me a questioning look. "He's not here to take me in. Zack knows I wouldn't do something unless I had a good reason. He's here because he needs me to do something off the books. He also knows this place has no listening devices."

"I have a question before he gives us a task that will get us killed. Did you know Kat was alive?" Antonio didn't leave room for Zack to get out of the question.

The look on Zack's face was all I needed to see. He had no clue Kat was alive. His jaw tightened, and his knuckles turned white from the grip on the beer bottle. "Antonio, if I had known Kat was alive, I would have told you. I received intel from the devil that the man you and Zane took out was the man who killed her."

The constant tapping on the keyboard had me looking over at Brock. "You want to inform the room of what you are doing, Brock?"

Brock looked from me to Zack. For a second, he looked like he wouldn't answer. I was friends with Sam, Brock's old boss, and had known Sam had a well-trained hacker working for him. I could only imagine what Brock was doing.

Zack spoke up. "You won't get in any trouble for whatever you're doing. You want to tell us what all the typing is about?"

Brock blew out a breath of air. "Well, I hacked a reconnaissance satellite and sent the video to the laptop."

"Wow, that took you long enough. I would have hacked it with a lot fewer keystrokes," Sophie announced with pride.

Brock's face flushed red. For an ex-Navy SEAL, he didn't seem so tough at the moment.

"I might also be talking to my fiancé. I needed to let her know I was okay."

"Pussy-whipped," Antonio coughed out.

"Makes me feel good to know the government satellites are so hackable." Zack looked irritated.

This conversation was heading off track. "Director San—uff!" Sophie elbowed me in the side. "Fine, the devil told me to go pick up Sophie today from her work. He didn't tell me why, just said all I needed to do was tell her she was being arrested for treason. Ten minutes after getting to her location, I was shocked to see Antonio show up. I took Sophie anyway and left him in Ft. Lauderdale. When we got on the plane, the devil informed me Sophie was my new partner."

Zack laughed. "That didn't throw up any red flags? You getting a partner?"

I hated working with partners, and the CIA knew I would do everything possible to get rid of one. A couple of times, I had killed them. They had turned out to be Russian spies. Still, I didn't like working with others. "Not funny, asshole."

"You can't say that," Sophie whispered.

"Say what?"

"You can't call the president an asshole."

"Sophie, Zack's an asshole."

"Let's get back on track," the asshole said. "I need to get back to DC."

I continued telling him how Sophie's sister was Kat, and the director had been using them against each other for years. The icing on the cake was that the director had told both Zack and Antonio that Kat was dead.

"This all lines up with what I was thinking and the information I've been gathering. Director Sanchez has been using the CIA for his personal gain. I need substantial evidence of his wrong-doing. I want him brought down."

"Can I kill him?" Sophie asked.

Zack shook his head. "I need him alive. This is off the books. He is still looking for you. I'm not sure who we can trust at the CIA. I need you to figure out what he's doing and bring him down."

Antonio had finally stopped pacing the living room. If he had kept pacing, he would have worn a hole in my imported armorial rug. He faced Zack. "We'll take the case, but I won't promise the director won't die at the end of this."

Sophie pointed at Antonio. "This is not your case. You can't cut me out."

"He isn't cutting us out," I explained. "I think Antonio and Brock should head back to Ft. Lauderdale and work on gathering intel. For some reason, the director wants Sophie. I think she saw something on one of the cases she worked for him, and now he wants her close. His dilemma is that she saw the picture of Kat. Now he doesn't have as much leverage. Sophie and I will head to another safe house nobody knows about." I gave my brother a pointed look. "I have a secure line where we are going and will have Sophie send you a secure message when we get to our location."

"I think we should come with you." Antonio didn't

seem pleased with leaving Sophie. It bothered me that he didn't trust me with her.

"I agree. What happens if you are surprised? Sophie doesn't have field training." Brock made a good point.

I looked over at Sophie. Under her confident exterior, I could see the worry in her eyes. "Fine. Antonio, you can come with us when we go to the charity event. Brock, I think you should go back to Ft. Lauderdale and work with the team to see what you can find for us. I don't want to use any contacts at the CIA. I'm not sure who we can trust."

Zack stood up. "I think you have everything squared away."

Even though it was under a bad circumstance, it was nice to see my brother. I stood up and gave him a one-armed hug.

As I was walking him to the door, I heard the distant sound of a helicopter. They found us a lot faster than I had thought they would. I looked over my shoulder to see Antonio pulling the gun from his holster. "How far out?" I demanded.

Brock's fingers were flying across the laptop. "Five minutes at the most. They are coming in fast."

"Sophie, come here." I ushered Sophie and my brother down the hall. I needed to get them into the safe room. We weren't entirely certain who was showing up or what they wanted.

Zack looked like he wanted to protest. He knew me well enough to know that I wouldn't listen. At the end of the hall, I removed a picture frame from the wall to expose a keypad. After punching in the ten-digit code, I heard the *click* of the panic room door latch. I escorted them into the adjoining bedroom. A door in the back of the bedroom closet stood ajar. I pushed them through the door before either of them had time to protest.

Needing to see what Brock and Antonio had found out, I headed back toward the living room. Antonio gave me a nod, and we got in place to take out the men coming for us.

4

SOPHIE

This day was getting to me. I had been taken into custody, forced into a job I didn't want, and had run from the Director of the CIA. Now, we were under attack.

"I absolutely hate being stuck in these rooms. I miss the days of taking down the bad guy," Zack grumbled. He was pacing back and forth, which was ridiculous since the room was four feet by four feet. He only took two strides before he hit the wall.

I had no clue what to talk about with the president. I gazed around the room for any form of computer or security system. I needed to see what was happening outside the panic room. The room had enough food for days. One side of the room was all shelf space lined with water bottles and canned food. I twisted to see what was behind me and saw a laptop.

Not wasting any time, I booted it up. A couple minutes later, I bypassed the password, and the welcome display flashed.

"Did you hack my brother's computer?"

"Yes"

"Hmmm."

I didn't have time to figure out what "hmmm" meant. I needed to see if everyone was okay. Antonio had become like an older brother who doesn't talk much, and Jessica would kill me if anything happened to Brock. It only took a couple minutes to get video of Brock watching from his computer. Zane had his gun pulled and was standing next to the front door. Antonio was by the back door with his weapon drawn.

The outside video showed the helicopter landing. Then a small figure stepped out. The sun was shining into the camera, so it was hard to see the person's face. When another little figure stepped out, I looked back at the other feed to see Brock running for the door with a panic-stricken look.

"What's going on? Who is that?" Zack demanded.

"I can't tell. The... oh, fuck."

The two shadowy figures came into full view. When I saw their faces, I immediately knew why Brock was panicking. It was his fiancée, Jessica, and my boss, Bridget. Then three beefy men stepped off the helicopter—Alex, Bridget's husband; Asher, Antonio's twin brother; and CJ. CJ and Asher had been dating for the past year and a half. I panned back to the cameras to make sure Antonio and Zane had lowered their guns. They had, but they looked angry.

I jumped up and headed for the door.

"We have to wait for them to release us from the outside. Zane has never given me the code."

Zane was probably worried Zack would leave after being placed in a safe house. "Well, I'm getting out of here. You can stay if you want." It took a couple seconds to retype the code I saw Zane type earlier. The light turned green. When the door swept open, Zane was there, reaching to put in the code. The look on his face said he was not happy.

"You want to tell me why you opened this door without waiting for us to clear the area?" Zane pointed at Zack. "How could you put yourself in danger like that?"

Zane needed to understand who was in charge. It sure as hell wasn't him. "I pulled up the video surveillance cameras, and we saw who was in the helicopter. Put your ego back in check." I dipped under his arm and headed toward the voices.

I could hear laughter in the kitchen. When I rounded the corner, Bridget saw me and ran over to wrap her arms around me. "I was so worried we wouldn't be able to get you back. Alex said he knew Agent Asshole and you would be okay. I couldn't handle losing you, so I had Jessica help me."

I heard Brock grunt from the other side of the room. "Jessica, why you are here? I told you we had everything under control."

Jessica's face turned a light shade of pink.

Alex pointed at Bridget. "I bet my wife is the one behind this. When I got word from my secretary that Bridget was taking my helicopter, Asher and CJ were in my office. So, we raced to the airport and boarded before they took off."

All eyes turned to Bridget. "I traced the IP back when you contacted Jessica." Bridget shrugged like it was no big deal.

Zane cleared his throat. "There is no way you traced the IP back to here. I have it looped around the world, and it would take even the best hacker a day to narrow down where we are."

For the first time in my life, I saw Bridget pale and look scared. She turned toward me. "You have to understand that I think of you like family."

I knew I wouldn't like the next words that came out of her mouth.

"When you said people would come after you because of the information you pulled on Jessica's family, I wanted to make sure you were okay. The necklace I gave you for your birthday has a tracker in it."

Before I had time to process her statement, Zack walked around the corner with his Secret Service agents.

Bridget elbowed me in the side. "Sophie, why is the President of the United States here?"

"Zack is Agent Asshole's brother."

"Well, I guess the plot to digitally destroy Agent Asshole should be postponed." Bridget seemed disappointed at not being able to destroy Zane.

Alex stepped forward and one-arm hugged the president. "It's been too long. Bridget, come here and meet Zack, a family friend."

Bridget went to the impressive men standing next to each other. "So, you are the lovely Bridget I've heard so much about."

Bridget gave her husband a questioning look. "Sorry, I can't say the same. Alex never mentioned knowing you before."

Zack let out a deep chuckle. "That's because it was Martha talking about her new daughter in-law and grandbaby." Zack stepped back, walked over to Asher, and gave him a hug. Then he reached out his hand toward CJ. "And you must be CJ. About time someone tamed Asher."

The next half hour was spent getting caught up.

"Well, I think it's time for me to head back to DC. Zane, stay safe, and take him down. I'm counting on you." With a wave of his hand, Zack left followed by his agents.

Everyone had migrated toward the living room. Somehow, I ended up sitting next to Zane on the couch. Bridget was sitting on Alex's lap in the chair next to the sofa.

"You finally going to tell me what the fuck is going on?" Bridget demanded.

How was I going to tell my two best friends that I had kept something so big from them? Zane must have noticed I was having issues. He reached over and squeezed my leg.

"I don't even know where to start."

"How about the beginning?" CJ replied.

I spent the next hour going over how my parents were killed and my sister kidnapped and how the Director of the CIA recruited me a few years later, saying he'd help me find my sister.

Bridget couldn't believe I had been working for the director all these years without telling her. I could tell she was hurt that I'd hid it from her. But, I had never trusted Director Sanchez and didn't want to bring Bridget or CJ into the mess. I had dreamed that, one day, they would get to meet my sister. But from the info

I saw earlier, I didn't know who my sister had turned into.

"Zane is going to help me find my sister."

"I will, Sophie, but I think Antonio needs to tell everyone how he is also tied into the mess."

Antonio looked pissed. If Zane hadn't called him out, he probably would have kept his secret with him until the day he died or had to tell everyone.

"Sophie's sister is my dead wife."

Alex had just taken a drink of beer and spit it out in surprise. Asher started laughing so hard that he had to grab his side in pain.

"I'm sorry. I could have sworn you said you had a wife, and she is dead. You better explain, or I will send a text to Dad, and then you will really need to explain what the fuck is going on." Alex looked hurt by the information.

"Kat and I married when we were on an assignment together. Right when we were heading home, she was killed in a café shooting. I didn't want to talk about it."

"Not even to me? How could you not tell me this? We tell each other everything," Asher said.

"Really? You want to go there? About telling each other everything?" Antonio didn't wait for a response. He got up and headed toward the kitchen. Asher hadn't told the family he was gay until he had started to date CJ.

The silence was thick in the room. So many secrets were coming to the surface, secrets that were put in place to keep people safe. Now that they were out, they seemed to hurt people, anyway.

"Sophie and I will head to another safe house." He pointed to the necklace around my neck. "Someone can take that with them until this case is over. I don't want any trackers on us. This time, we are going somewhere my brother doesn't even know about. Once we make it to the safe house, we will look into Yermushin and prepare ourselves for the fundraiser."

"You are not going anywhere without me." I hadn't even see Antonio reenter the room.

Zane ran his hand through his hair and let out a sigh. It had been a long day, and I could tell it was getting to him. It seemed like he was close to losing his temper. Not even realizing what I was doing, I reached over and squeezed his hand.

"Antonio, when we head to New York, we will contact you. We'll work with your office. You, Asher, and Brock, pull all the information you can, and we will contact you tomorrow. We have little time. I have a feeling Director Sanchez already has people heading this way. Sophie and I are leaving in ten minutes."

Alex nodded. "I have to agree with Zane. You need

to come with us. You were the last one to have contact with Kat. You can help us pull as much information as possible, so we can give it to Sophie and Zane. I also think we have something to talk about."

Jessica was the first to wrap me in a hug before they left. "I owe you my life. If there is anything, you need, let me know. Look on the positive side—seventy-five percent of kidnapping victims are killed within three hours. Your sister is still alive, and you will get her back."

Once everyone had left and it was only me and Zane, the house seemed to shrink.

5

ZANE

The sound of Sophie's stomach was a reminder that we hadn't eaten a meal today. Since I had collected her from the office this morning, we had been on the go. We needed food.

I looked over at Sophie. She was breathtaking. Her red hair was falling from her bun. Her white T-shirt was tight and accented her curves.

"In about ten miles, we'll stop and have dinner. I don't have food at the house we are heading to. We'll run out tomorrow and grab some groceries."

Sophie shifted in her seat. "If we stop at a store to pick up food, I can grab clothes and other things. It's been a long day."

"No."

"I need more than 'no.'"

"We have both had a long day. I need food, and from the sound of your stomach, you also need something to eat. I have clothes at the house you can wear, and then tomorrow, we can run to the store." I turned the SUV into the Greasy Spoon Diner.

The diner was showing its age. When Zack and I were kids, we spent summers up at the lake, and we would eat at the restaurant. Zack doesn't know I bought the cabin we used to go to when we were kids. It's the one place that reminds me of our mother.

The bell to the diner dinged when we opened the door. With one step into the diner, a tall, leggy blonde had me wrapped in her arms. "It's been too long, little Z."

I could feel Sophie stiffen behind me and heard her clear her throat. I stepped back from Georgia.

"Sophie, this is Georgia. Georgia, this is Sophie." Sophie reached out her hand to shake Georgia's. Georgia ignored her hand and engulfed her in a hug.

"Take a seat at the counter. Travis's flight landed a few minutes ago, and he's on his way here. It's been too long."

When we sat down at the counter, Sophie leaned into me. "I thought we were going into hiding at a safe house, not to find your ex-girlfriend." Sophie's knuckles were white from the grip she had on her fork. She looked close to using the fork to take Georgia out.

I would have let her stew in her jealousy for a few minutes, but Georgia was not having it. She must have overheard. She set a cup of coffee in front of Sophie and me. "Honey, you have nothing to worry about. We might live in the back hills of Virginia, but I'm not into incest. I married the man of my dreams. No need to marry my brother."

Sophie choked on her coffee. "Brother? I thought the president only had one sibling, according to the newspaper, and nobody ever sees that brother."

"Georgia's mom and my dad have had a relationship since my mother passed. Mary raised us, but she didn't like all the publicity that came with being married to the governor. We offered to go public and announce Georgia as our sister."

Georgia shook her head. "I love my life. The media was always in my brothers' lives. This one here somehow dropped off their radar years ago. I know who my brothers are. I don't need the media to tell me. Zack said you were in trouble and I wouldn't hear from you for a while. I take it you still haven't told him?"

I could tell Georgia didn't like that I was keeping things from Zack, but I disappeared to the cabin to escape the world. "I will tell him when he retires."

Before Georgia had a chance to respond, the bell dinged. At the sight of her husband, her face lit up with pure joy. Georgia had married one of my Navy SEAL friends. Travis had come to the cabin with me one summer, and they hit it off. Travis worked for a private security firm. I knew that if Sophie and I needed him, we could call.

Travis walked around the counter and wrapped Georgia in a hug and kiss that made my stomach roll. Sophie sighed. I looked over to see her staring at them. She looked lost in thought.

"Paying customers shouldn't have to watch you make out like your teenagers," I chided before Sophie elbowed me in the side.

Travis pulled back, and a grin spread across his face. "When you pay, I will listen to your demands. I don't think you or your brother have ever dropped a dime in here."

He was more than likely right. Zack and I had bought the house they lived in for their wedding gift. They both knew that if they ever needed a dime, we would do anything to help them.

Sophie reached out her hand to shake Travis's. "It's nice to meet you, Travis." He brought her hand to his lips and gave it a kiss. I might have growled at his antics, but I knew it was dumb since he was my sister's husband. He was testing to see what Sophie meant to me.

Sophie gave me a puzzled look. I didn't tell her I planned to murder him later for giving me crap.

While Travis and I were getting caught up, Georgia brought us our food. We had both ordered her chicken and waffles. Nobody could beat her cooking.

The noises coming out of Sophie's mouth were making my dick hard.

"Do you like it?"

"This is the best food I've ever had." She put another forkful of food into her mouth and closed her eyes to savor it. I had to look away before I embarrassed myself.

"Travis, do you still have cameras on the entrance leading out to the cabin?"

"Yes. I've added perimeter sensors to your cabin too."

Travis took care of the cabin when I wasn't around. With the missions we'd worked in the past, we both had people who would love to see us dead. He made sure no one could get to us.

Georgia had packed us a couple days' worth of food and an apple pie. We said our goodbyes to my sister and brother in-law. The cabin was a quick ten-minute drive from the diner.

"Zane, do you have a burner phone I can use?"

"Who do you need to call? Your boss and best friend already tracked you down." I wondered if she had a boyfriend she needed to contact.

Sophie shifted so she was facing me. "I need to call my landlord and ask her to take care of my cat, Jinx."

The tension in my back released. I tossed her one of my many burner phones.

SOPHIE

My landlord, Betty, would worry if she didn't see me come home for more than a couple of days. She would call the cops and have them put out a missing person report on me. I needed to heed this before it became something. On the fifth ring, she finally picked up.

I informed her that I was out of town with a friend and wouldn't be back for a week and asked if she would take care of Jinx. Betty said someone had been there earlier asking if she had seen me. She was worried and had already grabbed Jinx out of my apartment. She told me she had planned to call the cops if I hadn't come home by tonight.

"What's going on?" Zane asked. His voice was deep and rich. It made my insides melt when he talked.

I knew I needed to be straight with Zane because Director Sanchez was coming after both of us. I wasn't used to sharing this part of my life with anyone. For the last twenty-five years, I had dealt with Sanchez alone and hid it from everyone I knew because he asked me to. "Betty said someone scary was looking for me."

Zane shook his head. We turned down a gravel driveway lined with evergreen trees, and the smell of pine was refreshing. The SUV rolled to a stop in front of a small cabin. It was a complete contrast to the mansion we were at a few hours ago. When I went to get out, Zane grabbed my arm.

"I needed to disarm the landmines."

I laughed then looked at his face. He was serious. "Shouldn't you have done that before we drove into your yard?"

"Nah. I know where they are."

That wasn't too reassuring. Zane made a couple of clicks on his phone and nodded.

Who the fuck puts landmines around their house? This is crazy people stuff.

"Are you sure you got them all?"

Zane jumped out of the SUV and grabbed the bags of food from the back seat. When he was halfway up the drive, he turned. I hadn't made it out of the SUV yet. I wasn't sure if I would ever get out of the vehicle. But knowing I couldn't sit in the car all night, I got out and started toward the door. The sun was going down, and I was getting tired.

The inside of the cabin was warm and inviting. I expected a chair and TV, but Zane surprised me. The walls displayed photos of him, Zack, and Georgia. The living room looked into the kitchen, which had beautiful granite countertops and cherry cabinets.

"Not what you expected?"

It was scary how the man could read my mind.

"Run and take a shower. While you're in there, I will lay clothes out for you on the bed." Zane turned and started to put the food away.

A hot shower sounded like a good idea. I headed back to his bedroom to find a master bath. The marble shower was huge. It could fit at least four people. The rainfall shower head hanging from the ceiling was calling my name.

I spent close to a half hour in the shower. It was refreshing. I grabbed the fluffy white towel from the rack to go see what Zane had laid out for me. When I opened the door to the bedroom, I stopped in my tracks. Zane was in a pair of boxers, leaning over to dig through a drawer. The man had a light sheen of water on his body from a shower, and his muscles flexed as he rose. My mouth went dry. The man filled every fantasy my brain conjured.

Zane turned. His tight butt that made my mouth water.

"Like what you see?"

Cocky bastard. "I've seen better."

"Sure you have." He winked.

I couldn't take my eyes off him. When he found the clothes he wanted, he gave me another wink and left the room. The man knew what he was doing.

A shirt and a pair of sweats were waiting for me on the bed. Even though they were too big, it felt marvelous to change into some clean clothes.

When I went into the living room, Zane was sitting on the couch, watching TV. I sat next to him and fell asleep almost immediately.

The piercing noise of an alarm woke me. It must have also woken Zane. He leaped from the couch, bent down, and grabbed two guns from under the coffee table.

"Here. The safety is off. Shoot first. I will announce myself when I come back."

"Wait. You're going out alone? And who keeps guns under the coffee table?" A storm must have moved in after I had fallen asleep, because. I could hear the steady pounding of water hitting the log cabin.

"Yes, and I do. Stay."

Zane left through the front door, leaving me to wonder if he would be back or if was I going to die.

6
———
SOPHIE

Ten minutes and thirty-six seconds. That was how long it had been since Zane walked out the door. All I could hear was the rain that pummeled the roof and the thunder that shook the cabin. Trying to keep my mind off Zane getting killed by the intruder, I counted the seconds between the flash of lightning and the bang of the thunder. The lighting was close. I started to worry that Zane might get taken out by lightning or that the bad guy would make his way in. Zane might need help, and I was standing here with a gun pointed at a door that hasn't moved in ten minutes and fifty seconds. The thought of Zane getting killed made my stomach turn.

Between the ticking of the clock and the cracks of thunder, I knew Zane needed my help. I had never fired a gun before, but it couldn't be that hard to point and shoot. Not wanting to waste another second, I reached for the door handle and swung the door open. I had the gun in my other hand pointed forward. Outside, a shadowy figure stepped up the first stair to the house.

"Stop, or I'll shoot." My voice and hands were shaking, and I was having a hard time focusing on the target in front of me.

"Jesus, Sophie, what are you doing?" At the sound of Zane's voice, I dropped the gun and ran into his arms. "Well, if I knew this was all I had to do to get you in my arms, I would have sounded the alarm myself earlier."

Ever since losing my family, I was not good at showing emotion. Most of my life, I let the feelings build up inside me, and kept them there. I was feeling embarrassed by my reaction. I was so thrilled to see that he wasn't killed by an intruder. I peeled myself away from him and shifted toward the house. Zane grabbed my wrist and yanked me into his chest.

"It's okay to be frightened, Sophie. My stomach curled at the prospect of something happening to you. Let's move inside. I want to change out of my wet clothes."

Did someone find us? Did we need to move again? "What happened?"

Zane grabbed a towel from the cabinet in the entryway. "One of the perimeter sensors was tripped. I found deer tracks near the sensor. I need to reduce its sensitivity."

"How can we be assured that it was the deer that caused the alarm to go off?"

Zane pulled out a gadget with the same proportions as a smartphone. On the screen, it showed all the sensors and cameras.

"You going to explain why you left the house? I could have mistook you for an invader?" Anger dripped from his statement.

I could deal with his irritation. The knowledge of someone creeping up on me was another story.

"How long did you expect me to wait for you to come back? You left over ten minutes ago."

"Next time, pick up the phone, and call Antonio. I realize you worked for the CIA, but it was behind a computer. I served in the field. You don't have to worry about me."

It was difficult to hear the words coming out of Zane's mouth. While he was reprimanding me for going outside—which is what I think he was yelling about—he was slowly removing his wet shirt. The rain had been coming down in sheets, and water was running down his bare chest. All I could think about was running my tongue over his muscles.

Zane cocked his head to the side and gave me a knowing glance. "Are you listening, Sophie?"

"Yes. I can listen and watch at the same time. Continue, please." I had no shame. The man was drop-dead gorgeous. I wasn't looking for marriage. I just wanted to sleep with the man. Any woman would.

Zane was about to retort, but the buzz of the burner phone brought us out of our discussion. Zane walked over to his go-bag and snatched the phone.

"What?" A couple of clicks later, he had it on speaker phone.

Antonio's voice roared through the phone. "Sophie, did you keep any of the assignment data for the work you performed for Sanchez?" He went straight to the objective. I wasn't confident how to respond to the query. Director Sanchez had always ordered me to turn over all my analysis after each op. Knowing I didn't trust him, I had kept a copy. I wasn't sure how many laws I broke by maintaining government data on my external drive, but I figured it would send me to prison for a lengthy time.

"I suspect she did by the expression on her face. Sophie is wondering whether she should admit to keeping classified documents on her personal computer," Zane replied.

"Sophie, I guarantee you won't get in trouble. I might give you a kiss if you have them."

Zane growled back at Antonio.

"I kept a copy of every job."

"Do you have it with you?"

"No. Why do you need it?"

Antonio let out a sigh. "Brock and I have been looking into the ops you did. None of the cases you worked were on the books for the CIA. Everything you performed was contrary to US interests and made the director lots of wealth. We need confirmation, and if you have the data, it might make it easier to bring him down."

The knowledge that everything I worked on was for terrorists made my stomach curdle. Needing a second to myself, I sat down on the couch.

"I will call you right back and let you know where you can locate the intelligence." Zane didn't wait for Antonio to reply before he clicked the phone off.

The seat next to me on the couch sunk. "How old were you when you started working for the director?"

"A few years after my parents were assassinated. Sanchez showed up on my sixteenth birthday."

Before my parents were killed, I was heading to a gifted school. The school was extraordinarily expensive. My foster parents couldn't afford to send me. My IQ was off the chart, and I had a photographic memory.

"What did he have you do?"

"I was superb at puzzles and figuring out codes. Sanchez said he had a game for me to test what level I was at. Each time he came or called, he would have a new code for me to break. At the time, I didn't know what I was doing. The older I got, the more I looked at what I was doing. In the early days, he saw how I took to computers, so he supplied me with a computer and gave me network and coding books."

"Who was taking care of you during this time?"

"When I woke up in the hospital, and they told me about my parents and sister, a nice couple was waiting for me and took me home with them."

"Hmmm. So, none of your family claimed you?"

"My parents always said their family was dead, and we only had each other. That was all we ever needed."

"How were you not put in official foster care?"

"I never thought about it. Remembering that part of my life brings up too many bad memories."

I hadn't thought back to those days in some years. The more I thought about it, the less sense it made. The police should have turned me over to protective custody.

"What are you thinking about?"

"You're right. It makes little sense. The police came to my hospital room and took my statement when I woke up. My new parents were there before the police ever came. It was like the call was made before my parents..."

Zane must have caught track of my thinking. "Let's take this one step at a time. We need to find your sister before he moves her out of our grasp. After we get your sister back, we will see if Sanchez was responsible for your parents' deaths. Lastly, we turn the info over to my brother. Take my word for it. If he killed your parents, I will let you take the shot."

I'd waited years to figure out what happened to my family. Over the last day, I had discovered that everything I had known was false. "Won't your brother be mad for us not bringing him in?"

Zane let out a chuckle. "Let me worry about my brother. Where do you have the data hidden?"

It seemed so many people had conspired against me over the years. If I gave up this data, would I lose all the leverage I had against the man who might have hired people to kill my parents? I knew of one person I could trust more than anyone.

"Can I see the burner phone?"

For a second, it looked like I would not get what I wanted. Finally, Zane handed me the phone.

A couple of rings later, Bridget answered. "Whoever the fuck you are, do you know what fucking time it is? I have a baby and bar—"

"Shut up."

"Sophie?"

"Yes. I need you to do me a favor." I could hear the sheets rustling and Alex asking her something.

"Shoot."

"Antonio will show up once I call him. You know where my hiding spot is, right?" Bridget and I both had a place picked out where we kept things, and the other one knew where it was so that if we ever got in trouble, she could get rid of whatever was there.

"I have it and moved it."

I knew I could count on her.

"I need you to upload it to our server then hand it over to Brock and Antonio." Bridget and I also had a server not attached to White Hat. It was part of our doomsday plan.

"Already uploaded. Do you not fucking know who I am? That shit was uploaded and moved before Agent Asshole put you in the car."

"Thank you. I will talk to you soon." Not waiting for her reply, I clicked off the phone and handed it back to Zane.

"Why are you having the data uploaded?" He sounded irritated. I wasn't going by his plan. No way was I going to sit around and wait for Brock and Antonio to reanalyze all the data for the cases I worked.

I pointed at the phone in his hand. "You can tell

Antonio that Bridget has the hard drive with everything he needs."

Not needing to hear the conversation, I turned and headed for the kitchen. I needed something to drink and then a laptop. The wine cabinet next to the fridge was fully stocked. I reached for a bottle of red. I wasn't picky at the moment. A minute later, I had the liquid gold open, a filled wine glass in hand, and was on the hunt for a laptop.

Walking into the living room, I spotted a laptop laying on the coffee table. I swapped the wine bottle for the laptop.

A few seconds later, I bypassed Zane's password and bounced my IP around Russia. Once I knew my IP was off the grid, I logged into the server Bridget and I had and started the download of the data I'd collected over the years.

"You know, you could ask to use my laptop instead of hacking it." Zane's tone held a hint of amusement.

When I turned my head to reply, I was left speechless. He was standing in the hall, not wearing a shirt, and his sweatpants were hanging low on his hips.

7

SOPHIE

Working in the mountains had been a nice change of pace. The cool breeze blew across my skin. I took in a deep breath, and the smell of the pine trees made me appreciate the outdoors. The past few days had been a whirlwind of calls.

After three days of sifting through old case files, I was no closer to finding the connection between Sanchez and Yermushin. I cross-referenced all the cases I worked on with information from the CIA. Brock's finding was correct. The cases Sanchez had me work on were for his gain and not for the government. The money was leading back to the exact spot. But we couldn't find proof of what the director's end goal was.

I looked up from the laptop, taking in the landscape and the deer eating in the front yard. No wonder people come to the outdoors to get their mind back in order. It was calming to the soul. Zane had had a great idea to buy this place for a retreat from the real world.

"Find anything?" Zane's voice startled me. I needed to tie a bell around his neck.

I shook my head. An hour ago, he had asked me the same question. I was having a hard time keeping my hands off the man. The sexual tension was heavy in the little log cabin. I had spent most of today trying to separate myself from him. My self-control was running thin, and I was close to jumping the man's bones.

"If you need anything, call. I'm going to do a perimeter check."

I couldn't help but watch the man walk away. The jeans he wore accented his tight ass and I noticed he added an extra swagger to his walk.

The burner phone rang. I found it buried under a stack of papers on the table. "Hello?"

"You like checking out my ass?" His arrogant tone echoed through the phone. "I could feel your eyes on me."

"I don't need to inflate your ego any further." It was all I could think to say. I was caught.

I heard laughter through the phone before the line went dead. *Does that man not know how to say goodbye?*

Later, as I was lost in case files, I didn't hear Zane

approach. When he reached down and touched my shoulder, I about jumped out of the chair.

"Fuck! You need to stop sneaking up on me."

"Sorry. I was going to make dinner. What are you hungry for?"

When we ran out of the food his sister had supplied, we made another food run to the grocery store. The man wasn't only deadly with a gun, he could cook. Last night we had carbonara. The homemade noodles had melted in my mouth.

At the thought of food, my stomach grumbled. "Surprise me."

ZANE

Glancing at the timer, I stirred the jambalaya. The food was taking too long. *Why did I have to make something so time-consuming?* The woman out on the porch was driving me crazy. Cooking was helping me to keep my mind off of wanting to strip her naked and have my way with her.

I was reaching for the bowls in the top cabinet when I felt her eyes on me. I could always sense when she was near. She didn't think I knew when she was watching me, but I did. I heard her feet as she walked across the kitchen floor.

Her warm hands wrapped around my waist. I slowly grabbed one wrist at a time. I was close to losing control.

"Are you sure this is what you want?" Sophie's feminine shampoo was strong, and the smell beckoned me.

"Yes." Her voice was thick with lust.

Needing to have her in my arms, I flicked the switch on the stove. Our dinner could wait until later. I wanted Sophie spread across the bed.

I spun in her arms and nuzzled the delicate spot under her ear. A soft moan escaped her when I ran my tongue along her neckline.

"I've wanted to do that for the past three days," I said before taking a nip of her earlobe. A haggard breath escaped her mouth and her head tilted at an angle. I lowered my mouth to savor a kiss. "You taste better than I could ever imagine.

I slid my hands down her perfect body until my hands were on her tight ass. I spread my hands across the cheeks and grabbed her ass. When I went to pull her up against me, she jumped and wrapped her legs around my waist.

The need to possess her was so intense that it took over my control. I could barely think straight. Her fingers knotted behind my head. Our tongues danced. She tasted so pure and sweet. I headed down the hall with her wrapped around my body.

She nipped at my lip. Emerald green eyes met my gaze. Her lips were turned up into a smile. Needing to see what this woman looked like naked, I tossed her on the bed and ripped off my shirt. Sophie laid on the bed, her fiery red hair spread across the white comforter. Her eyes were focused only on me.

She bit down on her lip and ran her hand down her body. Then she slowly worked her tight jeans over her hips. I couldn't help but drink in her beauty. When she climbed off the bed, kneeled next to me, and took off her shirt, her beauty took my breath away.

"Gorgeous."

Sophie grasped at my belt, unclasped it, then pulled it loose. She didn't work the belt out of the loops. She needed me as much as I needed her and didn't want to wait any longer.

My pants hung low, and she ran her hand over the zipper, testing how hard I was. She worked her fingers into the waistband of my pants and tugged them down to my knees.

Once Sophie had my dick in her hands, she wrapped her pouty ruby lips around me. My vision went black for a second from the pure pleasure Sophie was inflicting with her mouth. I reached for the bedpost to keep my balance. A slight moan escaped her, sending vibrations through her throat.

"Sophie, look at me"

Sophie's green eyes opened. They were filled with arousal and lust. I gathered her hair in my hand, controlling her pace. My cock pulsed impatiently, needing release. When Sophie took my cock down her throat, I couldn't hold back much longer. I bit down on the inside of my mouth, trying to hold on. When Sophie cupped my balls, a gasp escaped my lips.

"Oh fuck, Sophie, I don't know how much longer I can hang on."

At my words, she picked up her pace, digging her nails into my butt, pulling me closer. Her velvety mouth was too much. I pulled out of it to gain control.

Sophie pulled me back into her mouth. She took me deep into her throat, causing her tonsils to massage the front of my cock. The sensation was too much, and I couldn't hold on any longer. I came, and Sophie worked to milk every last drop out of me.

I held on to the bedpost to keep from falling over. My legs were weak from the intense orgasm. When I had control over my body, I grabbed Sophie under the armpits and tossed her onto the bed. She was stunning.

"I can't wait to taste every inch of your body."

Sophie slowly dragged her hands down her naked body, stopping to play with her nipples. At the sight of her touching herself, my dick started to stir. Kicking my pants to the side, I crawled up the bed, kissing my way up her leg. When I teased her with a kiss on her inner thigh, Sophie let out a moan of protest. She tried to move to hurry me toward the place she wanted touched, but I continued to kiss and lick her inner thigh.

I worked my way to her clit, wrapped my lips around her nub, and started to suck. Sophie's heels dug into the bed, lifting her body up, trying to get more friction. Her soft gasp told me she was close. When I released her nub from my lips, she protested.

"I was so close. Don't stop."

"I don't want you to come yet."

I ignored the curse words that came from Sophie's mouth and slowly licked her slit. When I pressed two fingers into her velvety folds, she wrapped her legs around my head, trying to pull me in further and take control.

"Faster. Please." Her words came out in pants.

Wanting to feel her come apart on my tongue, I latched on to her nub and sucked while pumping my fingers into her. I flicked my tongue a couple of times.

"I'm coming. Fuck!" She exploded on my tongue.

Wanting to feel her fall apart again, I continued to suck on her clit. I pinched her tight nipple and rubbed it between my fingers."

"I need you, Zane. Please..."

The need in her voice had me licking my way up

her body in a straight line to her nipple. When I bit down gently to add a little pain, Sophie arched her back, pressing into me, wanting more.

I worked my way up to her lips and kissed her. She kissed me back with raw need. Her tongue swiped across my lips, looking for access. I opened them slightly, and she pressed herself to me.

"Please, Zane."

I was so wrapped up in the passion that I almost forgot about protection. "Hang on." I had to grab a condom.

"No." I could see the need in her eyes and body.

"I need to grab a condom."

She shook her head and pulled me into her embrace. "Don't need it. Are you clean? I want you without a condom."

I would need to take that information and store it for another day. The thought of being so close to Sophie made me harder than I thought possible.

Needing to feel her skin against mine, I rolled over and flipped Sophie on top of me. I wanted to watch her ride me. She squeaked in surprise at the quick change of position.

Sophie sat up and impaled herself on my hard length. I grasped her fingers in each hand, pulling her back down for a kiss. The desire to kiss and caress her curves was overwhelming.

Something more intense was forming between us. It was strong.

Sophie slowly rose and lowered herself on me, inching down until she was balls deep. It was pure bliss. She continued to rock back and forth. Emotions were flickering through her eyes. She shifted her hips down to get a slight friction on her clit.

"Goddamn, Sophie, move!" Her slow motion was driving me crazy. I grabbed her hips and increased her pace. She flung her head back and let out a moan. I pulled her down so I could suck on her nipple. The second my mouth wrapped around her nipple, I could feel her velvety folds massaging my cock.

Flipping Sophie over so I could take control, I flexed my hips, meeting heated flesh.

"Please," she begged. Her breathy moan almost caused me to come. "I need you."

With every thrust, a moan escaped her plump lips.

She pulled her knees up and wrapped her ankles around my back. It was the only sign I needed to drive her over the edge for a second time. She met each thrust halfway and tightened herself around my cock. Her breaths were erratic, mirroring the one-two punch in my own lungs.

Sophie screamed out my name as she went over the edge, loud and guttural. Her muscles pulsed, and she used me to drag out her climax. God, it felt like a silky explosion. I couldn't wait to do this again.

Her eyes flew open, full of emotion. Her red hair was spread across the pillow. I trapped each of her wrists above her head. Leaning down, I took a rosy pink tip of one breast into my mouth.

She rocked her hips, trying to push me deeper. Her moans were increasing, letting me know another climax was looming. I pushed her toward the pleasure, needing to see her come apart in my arms.

"Zane..."

Her voice came out raspy. With each thrust, her body bucked against me. She was close to crying out all over again. Every muscle tightened, and I couldn't hold back anymore. Our energy poured into each other with our loud cries.

Muscles finally going lax, the only thing on my mind was the woman under me.

Sophie groaned at the loss as I slid off her body, so I pulled her into my side.

What was happening between us was game-changing. I couldn't wait to explore it further. There was a good chance Sophie wasn't going to make it easy. I wouldn't have it any other way.

8

ZANE

The night before filtered through my head. Having Sophie under me was amazing. The thought of her climaxing to my touch had me hard. I reached over to the side of the bed to pull Sophie into me and noticed the bed was empty. I felt the sheets, and they were cold. She had left hours ago.

I reached for the pair of gray sweatpants lying on the floor and went to figure out where my redheaded angel had escaped to. She had another thing coming if she thought she could avoid me this easily.

The guest room door was closed. I opened the door, ready to give Sophie a piece of my mind for leaving the bed in the middle of the night. The sight I saw took my breath away. Sophie was sound asleep, with her red hair spread across the pillow. It looked so inviting. Just when I had decided to climb into bed with her, my phone rang.

I swore I would kill the person on the other side of that phone. It was too fucking early to be calling and bothering me. Leaving Sophie to sleep after the day we had yesterday, I walked out into the hall and closed the door.

"What?" Whoever was calling needed to get to the point.

"Is that any way to talk to your boss?" *How did the director get my burner number?* Sophie and I needed to leave the safe house. Our location was compromised.

"I told you I would take the case. When we find anything out, I will send you the intel." Like hell. I wouldn't send him anything. I thought he was up to his nose in bad dealings, and if it was the last thing I did, I would bring this man to his knees.

I overheard a shuffling on the other end of the line. "I need you to take Yermushin out. Bring Sophie back, and I will take care of her. I don't think she will be much help to you in the field. I will send another agent out to help you."

"Nope. I'm good."

"That wasn't a suggestion. I want Sophie back here today, or I will have your ass."

I walked back into the guest room and shook Sophie. When her dark green eyes landed on me, it was enough to take my breath away. I motioned that it was time to go. She seemed to understand and kick into high gear.

"I will report back when I have something." Not waiting to hear his reply, I clicked the phone off and stomped on it.

My go-bag was sitting on the bench next to the front door. I was ready to go. Sophie rounded the corner wearing a pair of my sweats and a T-shirt. I wanted to peel them off her body and head back to the bedroom. But, we needed to leave before any agents showed up. There was something we were missing in Sophie's tie to Sanchez.

"What's going on?" There was a slight shake to Sophie's voice.

"The director called. We need to get out of here in case he's figured out our location."

Sophie seemed to understand the urgency and followed me out to the garage. The garage was lined with high-end sports cars. I hadn't made it out here since we arrived at the cabin. The garage was three times the size of the house.

"Are these all yours?"

I've grown up with money. Sometimes it was hard to see what others see. I only saw a bunch of cars that went fast.

"Yes," I said tersely, not wanting to talk about my

family's money. I unlocked a luxury SUV. Sophie headed toward it. There was a very slim chance someone had made it into the garage. I didn't want to take any chances, so I pulled out a mirror to check under the cars for trackers or bombs. Once Sophie was inside the SUV, I did a quick check. The car was clean.

A few miles down the road, I pulled out a new burner phone and called Antonio. It rang once before his gruff voice came through the phone.

"Do you know how fucking early it is?" Antonio sounded as excited as I was when I got the call from the director bright and early. I glanced at the dashboard clock. It was 6:35 AM. It was fucking early.

I clicked the phone over to speaker, so I could concentrate on the road. "Sorry to wake you, Sleeping Beauty. Sophie and I left the safe house."

"What happened?" It seemed that once Antonio realized we had an issue, he perked up and forgot how god-awful early it was.

Sophie shifted in the seat next to me. She had been quiet since we got the call from the director.

"Sanchez called me this morning. He wants me to bring Sophie in and take on a partner for the rest of the op."

Antonio grunted on the other end of the line. "Do not take her in. Hold on a second."

I had no plans to take Sophie in. I would help her

find her sister and then tackle the chemistry between us. After a couple minutes, Antonio clicked back over.

"Do you know how early it is?" Brock grumbled through the phone.

"What did you find out last night? Sophie and I need to find a new location to lie low." Brock and Antonio's complaining was rubbing my nerves.

"Yermushin will be at the charity fundraiser tomorrow night in New York. Kat will be there with him."

"Can you get Sophie and me on the guest list?" It wouldn't be hard to get on the list. I could always pull the Zack card.

Brock complained about people underestimating him. "We were planning on calling you around nine to tell you the plan. You and Sophie head to Charlottesville airstrip. A plane will be waiting for you. Antonio and John, one of operatives that works for Blackwood Security, will meet you at White Manor Hotel and Spa in downtown New York. Once everyone is at the hotel, we will reconvene."

I needed Brock to do more digging. Things were not adding up. "Brock, I need you to look deeper into Sanchez and his connection to Sophie. I think he knew her before her parents died."

SOPHIE

The thought I might be in the same room as my sister brought butterflies to my stomach. For the past twenty years, I've been looking for her, and now I was days away from seeing her. The problem I was having was that my thoughts kept going back to last night.

It was one of the most mind-blowing nights I've ever had, and it could not happen again. The previous night was nothing more than a one-night stand. I had no future with any man. That was taken from me years ago. What happened with Zane couldn't happen again.

When I glanced in Zane's direction, I noticed that he kept looking in the review mirror. A black sedan had been a couple car lengths behind us for the past twenty miles.

"Why do you keep looking back?" I wish there was a *Spy Book for Dummies*. Even CliffsNotes would be helpful.

Zane pinched the bridge of his nose and let out a long sigh. "I need you to reach into the glove box and pull out a gun."

When I opened the glove box, I was shocked by its contents. It had everything an assassin would need. "Umm... which one do you want?"

"Hand me a Glock. Also, grab a grenade. We might need it."

Who the hell keeps grenades in their glove box? I

reached in and grabbed what I assumed was a Glock. It was black, and it looked similar to the one he had been carrying on his side for the past three days. I opened the clamp holding the grenade and pulled it out. Zane reached over and grabbed the weapon from my hand.

"You ready to tell me what is going on?"

Zane glanced in the review mirror. "The car behind us has been following us for the past twenty miles."

How do we know someone is following us for sure? "Maybe they are heading the same way we are. Ever think of that?"

"I've made three turns, causing us to completely change directions. There would be no reason for them to do the same."

"How about we outrun them or lose them?" *That seems like something a CIA agent would do. Don't they teach that in spy 101?*

Zane gave me a cocky smile. "We will stop and chat and see what they want. You will stay in the car, and if it turns bad, you will take off."

This fieldwork shit was getting old. I wanted to sit behind the computer and delete these men's identities, not go into a shootout. "Can you explain the plan?"

Zane veered off the side of the road. The car following us almost didn't see where we went, but they made a U-turn and came back at us. "I will talk to them. You stay here."

The black sedan came to a stop a few feet from us. Two men in black suits stepped out of the car. They were definitely CIA agents. Zane checked the magazine of his gun before he exited the vehicle.

I could hear murmurs from them talking. It sounded like they wanted to bring me in. When Zane responded, the agents looked upset with his reply. One of the agents reached for his side arm. Zane raised his gun, and squeezed the trigger. Two gunshots echoed through the air, both men dropped to the ground. Zane aimed at the car firing off two more shots taking out the front tires of the car.

Zane jumped back into the SUV, and we were on our way. He peeled out, leaving two agents and a car behind. I think it took a couple miles for me to get my voice to speak.

"You left two dead people back there." It wasn't a question. It was a statement.

Zane gave me a puzzled look and tapped his fingers on the leather steering wheel. "I didn't kill them. I merely made it harder for them to follow. They will both make a full recovery. It's their fault for thinking they could take me on. Both agents knew who I was and what I would do to keep you safe."

That made me feel a little easier, knowing we

didn't leave two dead bodies on the side of the road. It also made me feel better that Zane was still trying to protect me and get me back to my sister. He had no reason to defend me. His mission from his brother was to figure out what Director Sanchez was doing.

"Okay, how long before we make it to the airstrip?"

"It will be a little longer than I planned, since the car behind us has a grenade launcher pointed in our direction."

9

SOPHIE

"How can you be so fucking calm? They have a grenade launcher pointed at us!"

A large hand reached across the SUV and pulled my head down so that my face was in Zane's crotch.

A loud pop sounded behind us, followed by earth-shattering explosion fifty feet to the side of the car. The SUV swayed from the force of the blast. Zane quickly righted the SUV, all while pressing his foot down to get some distance.

I sat up. "Zane, this is not the moment to request a blowjob. They shot a fucking grenade at us." In the rearview mirror, I could see a billowing orange cloud from where the grenade had landed. The sedan was still behind us, keeping up with our SUV.

"A blowjob might reduce some of my tension.

They won't kill us. For some reason, the director wants you alive. We need to figure out what he wants with you." Zane made a quick turn to the right, causing the tires to screech across the asphalt, and the smell of burning rubber wafted into the SUV.

Once we made it around the corner, Zane pulled his Glock from his holster and rolled down the windows to fire bullets at the car behind us. They dodged the shots and pointed guns back at us.

"How are they tracking us?" My words came out as a whisper.

"Not sure. I assume they used the NSA satellites and tracked our facial images," he snapped, and she realized how stupid the question must have sounded. She used some of the equipment the CIA had when Sanchez asked her to do jobs. They weren't safe anywhere. Ninety-eight percent of your life is caught on video, according to Jessica.

Zane hit the hands-free button on the steering wheel and barked Brock's name. "Why are you not calling me on a burner phone."

"We're being chased."

Through the phone, I could hear the clicking of Brock's fingers on a keyboard. "Where the hell are you?" Brock demanded.

"We are on Interstate 64, heading east, toward the airstrip."

SOPHIE

There was a lengthy pause before Brock's voice came across the speakers. "I have eyes on you. You have company five miles ahead."

"I'm more worried about the assholes behind us." Shots rang out. The back window of the SUV shattered. Broken glass sprayed into the car. I could feel the shards hitting the back of my seat.

Zane gunned the engine. The SUV lurched forward.

"Are you guys alive?" Brock asked.

My mouth was dry, but somehow, I responded. "Yes."

"Take your next turn in a hundred feet."

Wanting to help, I sat up to assist with an extra set of eyes. I couldn't see anything up ahead except trees. *Is Brock sending us into a forest to go off-roading?* He needed to send a spy plane or something to blow these people up.

"Hold on!" Zane's demand had me grasping the side door handle with all of my might. Zane rounded the corner, and the force of it made it feel as if the car was about to roll. Somehow, we made it around the corner, all four tires hitting the ground with a thud.

The car behind us wasn't as lucky. When they took the corner, their vehicle flipped with the defining sound of metal crunching. Zane brought our vehicle to a screeching halt.

Is Zane losing his mind? Why is he stopping?

I heard Brock say, "Go!"

Zane protested. "We need a photo of these guys. If we can ID them, it will help us pull more information together."

Brock's voice came over the speakerphone. "Zane, we don't have time. They must have radioed the other men. Head straight to the airstrip. In a thousand feet, take a right. Head straight for about two miles."

We had broken through the trees. Corn was the only thing I could see for miles. "Brock, I think you are looking at the wrong satellite. I don't see a road up ahead."

I heard Zane chuckle. "He wants us to take a shortcut through the cornfield. Hold on to the dash. This might get a little bumpy."

Zane turned straight into the cornfield. Visibility went to zero. The SUV tore through the corn like butter.

"Are you sure we are going in the correct direction? I can't see a thing." It felt like we were driving in circles.

Zane pointed to the compass on the dashboard. I guess when you couldn't see the road, you followed a compass.

"In a hundred feet, you will come upon a road.

Take a right, and in sixty miles, you will be at the airstrip."

Satellite imagery would tell them where we were headed. "Are you sure the airstrip is safe? We might be going into a trap."

"Already took care of that. We have three different planes leaving at the same time as you guys. They are all flying to different locations. We have people dressed as you on the other plane, and we have new identities waiting for you on the plane. Antonio and John are on a flight to New York as we speak. We played a little shuffle game with their plane, too. I will keep an eye on the airstrip to make sure no one is heading that way."

Wow. Brock and Antonio were good at the spy game.

"I hope you loaded Antonio up with enough ammo for me also."

"Already done. Talk to you on the other side." Brock clicked the line off.

Zane continued down the highway for a sixty-mile stretch. We encountered no more agents. The wind whipping in the blown-out window of the SUV was not only a distraction, but it caused the cold to seep into the vehicle.

THE AIRPLANE SCREAMED MONEY. Before this morning's excursion, it had been years since I had been so frightened for my life or anyone else's. I'd heard stories about Antonio and Brock and how their missions would go. Hearing the story from my friends and being at the forefront were two different things. Somehow, it had worked out. We arrived at the airstrip and boarded the plane. The plane door was shut to the outside world, and we were one step closer to my sister.

Zane sat next to me in the plush leather seats. He reached over and grabbed my hand. It was still shaking. The last set of men who had come after us hadn't seemed to care if we lived or died. It was only thanks to Zane's driving skills and Brock's hacking skills, that we were safe for the moment.

A young blonde in a flight attendant's uniform approached us. "Is there anything I can get you, Mr. and Mrs. White?"

Brock was playing games again. "Our—"

Zane squeezed my hand. "Mrs. White will have red wine, and I will have a Scotch. Thank you." She turned on her heels and headed to the front galley kitchen.

"Why didn't you correct her?"

The man's actions irritated me. The game-playing was getting old, and we had only been on the mission for three days. I should have been grateful he was still helping me after getting shot at today.

Zane leaned his head back against the seat. "Brock didn't give our real names for a reason. Why change something he did to protect us?"

"You guys need to make a manual for these missions. It's hard when you haven't gone to spy school. The last mission I had for the director was setting up malware on the computer of the Prime Minister of Russia. It took me two days, and I had a clone of his communication funneling into a storage device. Oh, fuck, I forgot to give him the data I retrieved."

Zane was silent. He reached up and ran his hand through his scruff.

"You want to tell me why you are just now bringing up that op? This could be the reason he wants you. He might think you overheard or saw something and is cutting you out. Sanchez might think you turned on him, and he wants to bring you in to make it easier to find out what you know." Zane reached for his glass of Scotch and downed it in one gulp.

The director had contacted me before Jessica was kidnapped, and I had set up the malware to collect the data. But I hadn't yet logged in to pull the data off. I'd been dodging the devil's calls because I thought they were about Jessica. Zane was pretty smart for figuring that out so fast. Working on so many different projects, I sometimes forgot which ones were still going.

"When we get to the hotel, I'll find a computer and pull the data off. We can sift through the information and see what he was looking for."

The virus had been running for weeks. Hopefully, the server had enough storage capacity to have collected everything we needed. I could smack myself for forgetting.

"Can Bridget access the data?"

She could, but I didn't want to drag Bridget into trouble any further than I already had. She had a family to think about.

Zane reached over and grabbed me around the waist. It was effortless for him to pull me on to his lap. I knew the gesture was intimate, and I should have fought back. But, the day had been draining, and it felt good to be in his arms.

"Yes." I grabbed the cell phone and texted Bridget the information she needed to give Brock.

"No more talk about the op. I want to know why you left my bed last night."

I couldn't have this conversation sitting in his lap. The harder I tried to move, the tighter Zane's arms became.

"Go on, Red," Zane encouraged. "Tell me why."

"Why do you care? Last night was to scratch an itch."

"I highly doubt that's all it meant to you. If it were just an itch, you would have still been there in the morning."

This man was dangerous. He wanted to talk about emotions. Those are best kept buried in the deepest parts of your soul. If you let people in, they could hurt you.

"You could have any woman you wanted. Why are you pressing me?"

He squeezed my wrist and slowly dragged his thumb over the back of my arm. The touch felt so right. But, this man needed someone who wasn't damaged goods.

"I've traveled the world. I'm at a point in my life where I want to think about the future. One-night stands do not appeal to me anymore. Last night, we had a connection, and you ran. Why can't we see where it might go? I'm not saying we need to get married tomorrow."

"We can't have a future. When you find out what's wrong with me..." I was beyond frustrated. Every word he spoke made me think there was hope.

Zane shifted me on his lap so he could see my eyes. He ran his hand down my face. At his touch, my breathing increased, and my heart raced.

Holy shit! This man can make my blood boil.

"Sophie, has any man ever made you feel this chemistry? If I wanted a quick lay, I would get one. I don't. I want to be with you. Let's see where this goes. I don't know why you keep acting like you're damaged, when you are the most beautiful woman I've ever seen."

I was damaged. The man we were after took the choice of having kids away from me many years ago. No man would want to be with a woman who can't give him a son or daughter.

The pilot's voice came over the speaker, letting us know we needed to prepare for landing. I scurried of Zane's lap to the other seat.

He let out a sigh. "I will drop it for now, but this conversation is far from over."

10

ZANE

The day had been another cluster fuck and it wasn't doing anything for my mood. Tomorrow, we were going on a partial mission, and doing it blind. If everything went as planned, I would have Sophie in my bed tonight, her long legs wrapped around me.

The problem was that my gut told me something was wrong. My instincts were screaming to pull back and take the mission slow. Brock was tracking the CIA agents who had attacked us earlier, and they hadn't found our location. Nothing erroneous had surfaced. It was like the mission was too clean.

Being near to Sophie for the past week had my emotions running wild. I needed to go for a ten-mile run to release some of the tension that was building up.

Taking out the CIA agents early this week did nothing to settle my nerves. My gut told me something bad was coming, and we hadn't figured out what yet.

Brock was sifting through the data Sophie had stolen from the Russian Prime Minister's computer. Nothing was connected to Yermushin, so far.

Antonio was sitting in front of the computer, talking to Brock. Brock was in his conference room, surrounded by operatives. The team was trying to dig up as much intel as they could on Yermushin.

Sophie's fingers were flying across her keyboard. "This can't be true. This can't be true."

I leaned over Sophie's shoulder to see what she was looking at. "What can't be true?"

Deep down, I knew whatever she found would change the course of the op. The op was a snatch and grab. The harder mission would be taking Sanchez out.

When I leaned over to see what she found, I heard Brock yell "Fuck" through the computer's speakers.

A live broadcast of the director was running on the internet. "Turn it up."

"Sometime last week, my niece Sophie was kidnapped from her apartment in Ft. Lauderdale. I'm asking anyone who has any information to help find my miss—"

Sophie turned off the broadcast.

"Brock, are you getting this?" Was what he was

saying right? It made little sense. My pulse pounded. The director had put Sophie's face across all the TV stations. She couldn't leave the hotel or go to the charity event without someone seeing her.

"Yes. Sophie, did you have any clue he was your uncle?" Brock was pacing back and forth on the screen. His team of operatives were analyzing the newscast, taking down all the information as it flowed through the fucker's mouth.

Sophie had gone pale since the director's announcement. "If I'd known, don't you think I would have told you?" she snapped at Brock.

I dropped into the chair and ran a hand across my face. "So, the director tried throwing us a curve ball. It's time to find an alternative way to extract Kat from Yermushin."

"Do you think he's trying to stop us from going to the charity event?" Sophie asked, raising her eyebrows.

Antonio jumped from his chair and glared at Sophie. "We are getting my wife back tonight." Antonio slammed his hands against the table. "I don't care who comes with me. It's happening at sundown."

"Don't give me attitude. We are in this together. I've been searching for Kat for a long time. I just found out the man I've wanted to kill for years is my uncle. Fuck you." Sophie stormed out of the room.

"You need to watch it," I growled at Antonio.

Needing to find Sophie, I headed to the bedroom in the hotel suite. She was sitting on the bed, staring at a picture in her hand.

"Care if I come in?" Emotions were running high. I didn't want to upset Sophie any further.

Sophie waved her hand over the bed. "Sure. This is all my fault," Sophie whispered.

"How do you feel this is your fault?"

Sophie crossed her arms and glared at me. "If I would have researched Sanchez, I would have realized our connection. Who even knows if what he said is true? I don't understand why I never looked into him."

"He helped you when your parents died. He was an adult, and you were a teenager looking for answers."

Sophie's phone buzzed. Unknown caller flashed across the screen. She swiped the smartphone and put it on speaker. "Hello."

"You have nowhere to run. Time to come back. Everyone is looking for you. If you don't come in in the next four hours, I will tell the public that Antonio and Brock are behind the kidnapping. It will ruin their lives."

I motioned for her to keep talking and pointed to the living room. Sophie and I rushed back. Antonio and Brock were talking to each other on the computer. John was cleaning his gun.

"Why are you doing this?" Sophie asked, trying to keep Sanchez talking. "If you're really my uncle, why did you put me in foster care?"

"I didn't want to raise *two* brats. If you and your sister had been together, you would have caused me issues. The two of you might have figured out my plan."

At the sound of Sanchez's voice coming through the phone, the room went quiet except for the sound of Brock's fingers flying across the keyboard. I had a good feeling he was working on tracking the phone call. More than likely, the director was bouncing his signal around the globe.

Sophie was vibrating with anger. "If she lived with you, why is she working for Yermushin? Why would you make her work for the men who killed our family?"

Sanchez chuckled into the phone. "For having the IQ of a genius, you're pretty naive. She was too young to remember the faces. She is a trained killer. Ice does what I tell her."

Before I could stop her, Sophie threw the phone across the room. It hit the wall and shattered. I hope Brock found what he was looking for.

Sophie lost it when she realized she had destroyed the phone with the link we were tracing. I looked over at the computer screen where Brock was working, and he shook his head. I had figured it would be a long shot to trace the call.

"I'm sorry. I messed everything up again." Sophie was sitting with her head in her hands, crying.

I squatted down next to the chair. "Sophie, you need to pull yourself together. Yes, you are angry. You have every right to be. But, sitting here stewing over what ifs, won't fix anything. Let's go and talk with the team and see if Brock was able to trace the call."

"Okay, I'm ready, let's get my sister back."

Brock pushed his glasses up. "I couldn't trace the call. He was bouncing his signal all over the place. Steve just arrived with the files I had him steal from Sanchez's office. We have information on Kat."

"What information do you have?" Antonio growled. He had been on edge ever since he'd seen the picture of Kat.

"Since the director has been out all day, Steve could sneak into his office and retrieve the files from his safe. We might need POTUS to help clear his name when this is over.

I was nodding my head already. Zack owed me tons of favors for the things I'd done for him. He would take care of anything I needed. But it might not be necessary. I planned on bringing down the director and any other dirty officials.

Brock uploaded the file of scanned information to our computer. There was one on Kat and one on Sophie. "We could tap into Kat's phone line. The director called her right before he called you. Sanchez doesn't know we have this information. He told her he found out you were alive and was trying to get you back. Kat is taking the first flight out in the morning. Sanchez must think you will do as you're told."

Sophie shifted in her chair to get a better look at the documents on the screen. "We have to get her tonight and worry about Yermushin tomorrow. I want Kat back, and we can't have her fall into the director's hands."

"That was my next thing to pitch. I think we need to get her tonight. She lives in a house outside of Manhattan. There is one more thing." Brock paused as if he didn't know how to say what else he had found.

We didn't have time for games. "Spit it out," I demanded.

"She has a kid." A picture a beautiful four-year-old boy showed on the screen. He was the spitting image of his dad.

Antonio leaped from his seat. "You're telling me that low-life piece of shit kept me from my wife and *son*? I will rip his heart out and watch him die a slow painful death."

"That was graphic. Before you go hulk and turn green, let's talk our plan through. I agree we go in late tonight. We'll have the dark as our cover. If someone is watching her, we'll need to be quick."

The mission to take Kat at the charity event would have been more straightforward. We planned to lure her into a hall or bathroom, explain the situation, and get the fuck out. Now, the mission was to go into a residential neighborhood. Her house was more than likely being monitored by Sanchez or her current employer, Yermushin.

Mia's voice came across the computer. "From glancing over the file, Kat is a trained killer. She thinks she is doing jobs for the United States. Instead, she's working the director's hit list. Last month, she tried to get out. She told him she was done. He threated to take Antonio Jr. away and ruin her. If she wanted out, she had to do one last job. I sent you the schematics of the house and neighborhood."

The address and map appeared on the monitor. Sophie worked on bringing up any cameras we could find to see if we could figure out our blind spots.

"Holy shit." Brock sounded like he saw an alien.

"What did you find?" I asked.

"Sophie, you never told us who your family was."

Sophie looked confused. "My parents were professors at a college. We were nobody famous."

Two images appeared on the screen. I recognized Joe and Lexi Johnston. They had been the wealthiest oil family around. They had died in a car accident years ago.

"Your grandparents were Joe and Lexi Johnston. When they died, their fortune went to your parents. Nothing went to Sanchez. From the look of it, your grandfather had an affair, and Sanchez was the outcome. He paid Sanchez's mom to go away. When your parents died, everything went into an ironclad trust in your sister's and your name. It looks like Sanchez has been taking the money from your trust. If you or your sister die, it goes to a charity, and then he wouldn't get anything."

"Mom said our grandparents were dead. I never thought to look into them. Sanchez has a different last name, and I never looked into my mom's last name."

Now it made sense why he needed her alive, and keeping the sisters apart made it easier for him as well. They would've talked and maybe looked into their background. Instead, Sophie tried to track down her sister's location, being fed intel from a man that didn't want her to be found. Who knows what information he was feeding Kat?

Coming up with a game plan filled our afternoon. I didn't want Sophie to come on the mission. It would be dangerous. But she wasn't taking 'no' for an answer. I didn't want her going off on her own and causing more problems.

We still had a few hours before the sun went down. I had an idea about how to keep Sophie's and my mind off what was going on. There was something about Sophie that was irresistible.

11

SOPHIE

The room cleared after the briefing. John and Antonio left to grab food. The tension was thick between Zane and me. I couldn't think about anything except getting my sister back. Twenty-five years we'd been apart, and in five hours, I would see her again. Not only was I getting my sister back, but I would also meet my nephew for the first time.

Needing to create space between Zane and me, I reached for the door connecting our rooms. The hotel room was like nothing I had seen before. These rooms were meant for royalty, and they weren't going cheap on the decor. The walls had gold-plated artwork. I ran my hand across the bedspread. It was soft and inviting. The thread count had to be higher than anything I could imagine.

The bathroom was the size of my apartment. The walls were lined with white marble. In the corner sat a tub that would fit ten people. I was having a hard time deciding between the shower, with ten jets sticking out of the wall and ceiling, or lying in the tub and pulling up a good book on my phone.

I was so entranced by the finishings in the bathroom that I didn't hear Zane walk in. He wrapped his arms around my body. I could feel his hard-muscled chest against my back. His calloused hands ran up and down my arms, sending a shiver through my body.

When his lips touched my neck, I couldn't hold back the sigh. "We shouldn't be doing this."

"We both need it." It might help relieve the stress and the worry for an hour. But, I'd told myself I wasn't going to end up back in bed with him.

I couldn't think straight when his hand slid down the front of my jeans. Zane slowly licked the back of my ear. "Your lips might lie, but your body tells me everything I need to know. Your pussy is dripping with need."

When his finger found my clit, I leaned farther into his touch, resting the back of my head against his shoulder. Zane dragged a finger up my body to my tight nipple. I couldn't take it anymore.

I turned in his arms and dropped to my knees. The zipper wouldn't go fast enough. I shoved his pants and boxers down to his thighs. The second his cock sprang free, I grasped it in my hands. It had been hard not to think about the sexual tension between us the last few days. No matter how hard I tried, the sharp arousal kept clawing at my insides.

Needing to give him the pleasure he'd given me, I wrapped my mouth around him.

ZANE

The warm velvet of her mouth wrapped around my length and almost sent me over. Nothing could compare to how I felt in her mouth. I had to grab the wall to keep my balance. I lowered my free hand and twined it in her hair, controlling her speed. When those emerald eyes looked up, I was lost in her gaze. One hand moved up and cupped my balls and the other wrapped around me, pulling me in deeper. I could feel my member hitting the back of her throat.

With each drag, she went deeper, and she hummed, creating a vibration I'd never felt before. I'd had hummers from women who were skilled, but they were nothing compared to Sophie. I couldn't take it much longer. The feeling of needing her was too strong. I grabbed her under the armpits to pull her up. Her eyes were heavy with need.

"Fuck. You're undoing me."

A sly smile creeped across her face. She knew what she was doing. I had her undressed in a few seconds.

"Stunning." She was spread across the white bedding, her red hair going in every direction.

"You going to stand there all day or come take care of me?"

I was on edge from the blowjob. I took my time kissing up her body. Her skin felt like satin under my touch. I kissed my way up the inside of her leg until I got to her clit. I clamped down and started to suck. Her body arched with desire.

When I nipped, adding a mixture of pain and pleasure, it sent her over the edge. Seeing her come apart, I couldn't take it anymore.

I flipped her on her stomach, and in one thrust, I was buried deep inside her. She felt like heaven. The gasp of surprise was followed by a purr. With each stroke, I was filled with the need to possess her.

"Goddamn, Red." Our movement was synced. She met each thrust with need.

Sophie called out my name as she climaxed, loud enough for any adjoining rooms to hear. Her velvety folds pulsed. I loved it. She continued to rock her hips, each thrust getting me closer to my climax.

When she started to slow down, I spanked her ass. Her muscles clenched with the hit and her movement increased. She was nearing another climax. I hurried my thrusts, meeting her needs. We both climaxed at the same time, going over the edge.

When I rolled us both over, I took her lips in mine, and the kiss was spellbinding. I pulled her body to mine. It took a while for both of us to start breathing regularly.

When we seemed to be coming back to reality, she crushed the mood in five words. "Thanks. You can leave now."

We had just had mind-blowing sex, and she was kicking me out of her room. "No."

Sophie wrapped the blanket around her tighter and headed for the bathroom. "We agreed to relieve the tension. Tension has been relieved. Thank you."

"It was more than that, and you know it."

She still didn't believe this was more than a fuck to me. We had chemistry outside of the bedroom.

"Out." I could see a light sheen to her eyes. She was struggling with what was between us, and I needed to give her time. I grabbed my stuff and headed toward the door.

"Sophie."

When she looked up at me, tears were running down her face. She needed time, and I was going to give it to her.

"This is far from over."

Before she had time to give me another one of her lame responses, I shut the door. John and Antonio had gone down to the bar to get food. I normally didn't drink before a mission, but Sophie had my emotions all over the place.

The guys were propped up at the bar, eating hamburgers, when I got there. Antonio raised his brow in question. He knew I wanted to spend time with Sophie. When I shook my head, he didn't ask another question.

"What can I get you?" the bartender asked before I even sat down.

We were the only people in the restaurant. "Burger and two fingers of your most expensive Scotch. Put it on his tab." I pointed over to Antonio.

"Want to explain why I'm the brunt of your mood?"

Not wanting to talk about what happened, I changed the subject. "I think we should send the women back to Ft. Lauderdale right away. After the mission, we drive them straight to the airport. We can take down Sanchez ourselves."

Antonio popped a fry in his mouth. "From the look of frustration on your face, you are already in the doghouse. I don't think sending Sophie away and not letting her get her vengeance is going to help you."

He had a good point, but pissing her off to keep her

alive might be the correct thing to do. The bartender set the hundred-dollar glass of Scotch in front of me. Needing to feel the burn of the alcohol running down my throat, I drank the Scotch in one gulp. I pointed to the glass again.

"I won't let you go on the mission if you are drunk. We are going after my wife and kid."

"Not planning on getting drunk. I'm having one more. I'll sip the next one."

John had been quiet since we arrived. I always thought Antonio was a man of few words, but John was pure silence.

"John, do you think we should send the women back?"

He leaned forward resting his hands on the bar top. "I would do anything to protect the women I love, but they don't always listen. Sometimes, keeping them where you can see them is better than not knowing."

The words sounded like they were coming from experience. We'd go in tonight, get Kat and Antonio Jr., meet at the hotel room, and come up with our next game plan. John was right. If I tried to make Sophie stay back while we went after Kat, she would find a way to show up. She'd been looking for her sister for years, and nobody would hold her back.

"Here's the question of the hour. When the

mission is complete, where are you headed?" Antonio asked.

I'd thought about that a lot of over the past few days. I had more than enough money in the bank not to work another day of my life. The CIA missions were starting to get old. Maybe it was time to settle down.

"Are you hiring?"

Antonio must not have expected that response. Or maybe he did. A sly grin spread across his face. "You're welcome to come work for me. Since you're rich, I don't have to pay you much."

Asshole. With an idea forming in my mind about how to wear Sophie down, a little of the tension rolled off my back. A run would remove the last of the tension.

"Thanks for the job. Keep this between us for a while. I want to be the one to talk to Sophie about it. I'm going to go for a quick run. See you guys in an hour."

12

SOPHIE

Kicking Zane out of the room was one of the hardest things I'd done in a long time. Every time we were together, the feelings grew stronger. I needed to cut ties before I got my heart ripped out. There was no way Zane would want to be with me once he found out I couldn't have kids. Men like Zane need to continue their family line.

Thinking I could sleep with a man like Zane and not become attached was stupid. It was supposed to be a fling. Screw the man and get him out of my system. The problem was that every time we were together, he crept into my heart a little bit.

I closed my eyes and took a deep breath. I needed to get my emotions under control. We were meeting in Zane's room in fifteen minutes. But when I closed my eyes, I saw his shaken look, which turned into disappointment. I could handle anger. Disappointment made my stomach curdle.

It was hard not to fall into bed with the man. His muscles had muscles. His scruff. His tongue. I had to shake my head to get rid of the images of Zane that kept coming back, leaving my body in a permanently heightened state.

Glancing at the clock, I saw I was running behind. The X-rated images of Zane had my brain going out of control. I wanted to kill him and keep him all at the same time. I knew I would never get to have him in my life permanently. For starters, his family was one of the most prominent families around. I grew up in foster care and spent my time hacking into criminals' computers. Prestigious families like Zane's expect to have biological kids. That choice was taken from me years ago and I chose not to burden others with my pain.

Since Zane's room was next to mine, we had a connecting door. Every step toward the door made it feel as if my feet were sinking in quicksand. I knew I needed to face Zane. He was helping me get Kat back. But, when I reached for the door handle, the door swung open with an angry Zane on the other side. Damn, that man was hot even when he was angry. It seemed as if he could read my mind, as his angry scowl turned into a cocky grin.

"Sophie, it's about time you join us."

I was a couple of minutes late. The man knew I was on the other side of the door. If it was an emergency, he could have knocked or come over. Not justifying his answer with a response, I rolled my eyes and brushed past him into his hotel suite.

Antonio looked up from checking his gun and nodded.

Needing space from Zane, I sat next to Antonio. With a motion of Zane's hand, the big bad Antonio vacated the spot. *Traitor*. Zane's muscular scent was intoxicating and made it hard to concentrate on the mission, and getting Kat back was one of the most critical missions of my life.

The tension in the room was high. I wanted Kat back, and Antonio was going after his supposedly dead wife. Zane cleared his throat. It was time to start the briefing. He started the discussion with a recap of the new information regarding Sanchez. I was still numb from the news that he was our legal guardian and was using us to access our alleged trust fund.

When Zane finished the briefing, he asked Brock, "Do you or your team have anything else to add?"

I was embarrassed to be around Brock and his team.

We had spent years hacking and taking people down. I considered myself one of the best hackers around. I wasn't being cocky. I was good, but for some reason, when it came to my life, I didn't investigate or use the tools around me.

At the sound of Brock's voice, I looked up at the screen. He was chewing a piece of licorice. I swore the man had stock in a licorice company with how much of it he ate. "We've been monitoring the house using satellite cameras, and we borrowed the feed of one of the neighbor's cameras."

Zane leaned back in the chair and ran his hand over his scruff. "Any changes."

"The house next door has two guards in it. I got a facial recognition on them. They are guns for hire, so they could work for either Yermushin or Sanchez. They don't have any other surveillance on her. I got the camera feed they have pointed at her house. I took the feed and made a loop. When you head their way, I will switch over to the feed I created."

I could tell Zane was thinking about something. He had a look of determination. "Once we have Kat, you need to erase the footage and any tampering you did."

I had to hold back a chuckle. The look on Brock's face was priceless. Zane hadn't worked with him before. He was good and would've covered his steps.

Brock's voice turned deadly. "You work in the field. I work behind the computer making sure you don't get killed. I know how to do my job. Never question my work."

Zane held up his hands in defeat. "Sorry, man. I'm used to working with analysts or on my own."

"Don't worry about it. I planted a virus in the system. No one will know the footage is different. The drives will automatically DOD wipe, and the data on the drives will not be able to be retrieved."

Mia chimed into the video conference. "The guards ordered takeout. We had one of our contacts in New York drop sleeping pills in the food. They will be out cold for the next few hours. You need to be gone."

"Let's head out in fifteen minutes. I need a moment with Sophie." The room cleared, and our connection to Brock went black.

Zane's dark eyes leveled me with an intensity that almost knocked me over. I could tell he was still fuming about me kicking him out of my room earlier. His desire for me also shone in his eyes. He raked his eyes over my body, and I knew it wasn't to make sure I was wearing proper clothes for the mission.

"I wish you would consider staying back." There was a hint of hope in his voice.

There was no way I was staying back on this mission. I had been away from Kat for too long, and if he tried to keep me away, I would just find an alternate way to go.

"I know." I shrugged my shoulders, not caring about what he wanted. "I'm going anyway. Would you stay back if it was your brother?"

Zane walked over and wrapped me in his arms. "I don't want you to get hurt. I know you feel what is going on between us."

I couldn't think when Zane was so close. I pushed on his chest to get room. I needed to get my mind off Zane. When he was close, all I could think about was being with him, and that could never happen again.

"The only thing between us is lust."

"Bullshit."

"Zane, there can never be more, and we need to stop this before one of us gets hurt." I knew it would be me that ended up heart-broken. It was already tearing me apart to push him away, and if we spent much more time together, it would be even harder.

He ran his hand though his scruff, letting out a growl. "Whatever is holding you back, we can get through it, whatever it is. Once we get Kat back tonight, we will sit down and figure it out."

Kat is all I needed. Once I got her back, I would be on my way back to Ft. Lauderdale with my sister, and Zane would be on his way back to DC.

"You think tomorrow you can go your separate way and forget about what is between us." At the shake of my head, he said, "I see it in your eyes. I'm not sure what is between us, but it is not ending tonight."

When I went to respond, the hotel door swung open, and Antonio and John walked back in. They were both dressed in full tactical gear. Antonio had a look of determination on his face. This mission was as vital to him as it was to me. He was going after his wife and a son he had never met.

"Time to roll," Antonio grunted and motioned toward the door.

Zane grabbed his sig and holstered it. As he walked toward the door, he stopped and whispered in my ear. "Don't even think we are close to being done."

Before I had time to respond, he was heading out the door, and Antonio was giving me an irritated look for dragging my feet.

KAT

I'd spent years mourning my family only to find out my sister was alive. Nothing made sense. Why hadn't Juan called and told me before going on TV? I looked down at my phone, noticing the thirteen missed calls. Okay, I hadn't answered his calls before the broadcast.

What if they didn't find her and I had to go through losing my sister all over again? I've had so much heartache. Every time I looked at Antonio Jr., my heart ached for the only man I'd ever loved.

I wanted out of the agency. When I was younger and had so much anger about losing my family, it was easy to put it into the fieldwork.

Juan told me that if I did this one last favor, he would help me find the people behind Antonio's death. I hated being around these men. What Juan didn't know was that I'd been watching his dealings. He'd been sending me on cases for the last five years, saying I was helping the United States government. But, the recent case was too much. He wanted me to take out a family. Every case he had me work, I researched. If I didn't feel like the people deserved it, I sent them to a little town in Africa. One day I would have to visit the city that was comprised of the people I'd saved from Juan's corruption. I paid for them to go away and faked their deaths.

I didn't plan on letting Yermushin get away with selling the nuclear codes he had. The problem was that the deal was going down at the charity event tomorrow. I was trying to come up with a plan to stop it or change out the codes somehow. The only way Yermushin could have gotten the codes were from Juan, but now he was sending a plane to take Antonio and me back to Ft Lauderdale tomorrow morning to help find my sister.

Yermushin thought that, after the codes were sold, he was done working for Juan. Juan's primary plan was for the nuclear codes to be sold, and the money to be put into his account. Yermushin thought I was there as his bodyguard, but my primary mission was to take him out.

How could my sister possibly be alive after all these years? How could she not come looking for me? Maybe Juan had figured out my plan and was doing this so I was unable to go to the charity event tomorrow night. The codes were on a black thumb drive. Perhaps I'd go to the charity event and fly home afterward. I needed to get the thumb drive before it was sold to North Korea.

"Mommy, why do you look so sad?" Antonio was my light. I'd had so many dark days in my life, but he was the one thing that kept me going. I hated taking him on missions. This one had lasted a few months. Yermushin had to gain trust with the North Koreans. No way was I going to be away from my son for a few months. Gini, one of my nannies growing up, had retired to New York. She had been helping me when I needed to go assist Yermushin.

Juan had also insisted on the bodyguard living next door. I didn't understand why he thought a trained assassin needed to have muscle. I had my trusted M24 sniper rifle.

I reached down and pulled Antonio into my lap. "I'm not sad. I was trying to figure out a plan."

"I saw Uncle Juan on TV. Do I really have another Aunty?" For a four-year-old, he picked up way more than he should. He always talked about his friends having big families and asked when we would get a bigger one. "I'm not sure honey. I need to find out more information."

Antonio jumped down from my lap. "I hope so. You seem so lonely. Maybe aunty will have kids too."

"Come on kiddo, it's time for bed."

Antonio ran down the hall to the bathroom. I could hear the water running. So many questions about Sophie roamed through my head. *Would Sophie have kids? Does she know I'm alive and if so why hasn't she ever looked for me?*

"Mommy, are you coming?"

I was so lost in thought, I hadn't heard Antonio head to his room. When I walked in he was already under his Marvel bedspread. Next to the bed sat a picture of Antonio's dad. No matter how many times I looked at it, he still took my breath away.

"Good night, kiddo." I leaned down and kissed his forehead. He is growing so fast and looks so much like his father. Antonio would be so proud of him.

When I was about to flick the light off, Antonio asked a question that made my heart break.

"Mommy, if aunty Sophie is still alive. Do you think daddy is?"

How many nights had I laid in bed hoping to see his eyes one more time or lay in his arms?

"No, I know daddy is dead for a fact."

Needing to suppress the thoughts of Antonio. I grabbed a glass of wine and sat down with my e-reader. Nothing like a good book to distract you from a wondering mind.

The two main characters were running for their lives when a loud pounding on the front door startled me. I glanced at the clock and saw it was past ten. Who the hell would show up at this time? For the last two hours, I had been trying to fall asleep. Sophie kept coming to the forefront of my brain.

Another series of knocks sounded on the door. I wasn't in the mood to deal with Yermushin's or Sanchez's men. This was my private sanctuary. I had done little with the place since we moved in. The walls were still generic white and not decorated. Once this job was over, we would move again. The next time will be the last. One assignment, and I was done. One assignment until I went after the man that killed my one true love. This constant moving wasn't fair to Antonio, and he would enter kindergarten soon. I hadn't figured out where we were going yet.

When I looked through the peephole, I couldn't

see anything. I grabbed the gun from under the end table. I'd never trusted Yermushin or his men. I'd done jobs for him in the past, and it was time to part ways. After I took him down, I would need to go on the run. I shook my head trying to get my thoughts back in order.

I opened the door. *Was I still dreaming?* Antonio was standing in front of me, his forest green eyes seeing straight into my soul. My eyes trailed downward, not being able to help looking over the man who lived only in my fantasies, for the past five years. His black shirt molded against his chest, showing raw masculinity. When my eyes sprung back up and looked at his face, I was still not sure what I was seeing, as his lips turned up into a cocky smile. He knew I was checking him out. I didn't move a muscle hoping everything would stand still, when movement to the right had me looking to see who was with him.

Sophie -- it might've been twenty-five years, but I would recognize my sister anywhere. Her red hair was tied up in a bun. She had slight wrinkles next to her eyes, showing years of stress. Like Antonio, Sophie was dressed in all black. She looked nervous and excited, her hands twitching at her sides wanting to reach out. Not one hundred percent sure my mind wasn't playing tricks on me, I tightened my grip around the 9mm in my hand.

"Kitty Kat, you need to let us in."

When Antonio's deep hypnotic voice registered in my mind, I knew he was real and it was too much to take in. How could this be possible? He was dead. He died in my arms. My brain could not comprehend what was going on. The world went dark, and my body dropped.

13

SOPHIE

Over the years, I had imagined different scenarios of seeing Kat for the first time. Her passing out and almost hitting her head was not one of them. But, she more than likely never expected to see her dead husband and dead sister again.

Antonio grabbed Kat from Zane's arms. When Kat hadn't answered the door immediately, Zane had gone around the house and picked the lock on the back door. He was walking up behind Kat when she collapsed and was able to catch her before she hit the ground.

"Someone grab a cold cloth," Antonio demanded.

I ran into the kitchen to grab a cloth. There, I came face to face with a three-and-a-half foot mini Antonio. He was the spitting image of his dad.

"You look like my dead aunt. Are you a ghost?"

It took everything in me not to burst out laughing. The little guy was so serious with his question. He continued to look up at me with his crystal blue eyes.

"I'm your aunt, not a ghost. I need your help. Can you find me a rag?"

Little Antonio opened a drawer and handed me a dishcloth. I was still in shock over being an aunt, and seeing him in person was throwing me. After running the rag under the cold water, I reached down and drew him into my arms.

"Hey, buddy. Let's head into the living room and check on your mom."

"Okay." He grabbed his blankie and walked toward the living room.

Since I was concentrating on getting back to Kat, I didn't notice that the mini Antonio had stopped dead in front of me. I tripped and flew forward. Like always, my knight in shining armor was there to catch me. Could this man do nothing wrong? He always seemed to be in the right place at the right time.

When I was finally standing back up, I looked down to see why the little guy had stopped. He was staring at Antonio, and the big brute was staring back. It seemed like the big, bad Antonio's eyes were glossy. I wouldn't want to be the one to point out that the big, bad ex-military guy was close to crying.

I was close to crying, myself. It was one of the most

beautiful sights—a son and his dad getting to meet each other for the first time. I wish Kat were awake to see this.

"You look like my dad, but Mommy said Daddy died." His bottom lip was quivering. "What's wrong with my mommy?"

Antonio squatted down. "I'm your dad. Your mommy was told lies. Why don't you come he—"

The little guy flew through the living room and jumped into his dad's arms. I couldn't hold back anymore and tears were running down my face.

When I looked at Antonio, he had tears running down his face too. He didn't care how it looked. He had finally found his wife and kid. Under the tears, you could see the anguish from missing so many years with his family.

A grumble from the couch had everyone turning their eyes from the scene of a dad and son reunited.

"How...?" Kat choked out. She also had tears running down her cheeks. "You died in my arms."

With his son in his arms, Antonio rushed over to where his wife was laying. "Hey, Kitty Kat."

"He said you were dead, and I..." She was crying so hard that she couldn't get her words out.

The reunion on the couch was intimate. I needed to look away. I felt like I was intruding on their private moment. When Zane wrapped his arms around me, it felt good to have someone there to comfort me. I would hold onto this moment for the rest of my life. Each time he wrapped his arms around me, it made it harder to walk away.

Kat finally calmed down and released her grip on Antonio. When her eyes swung to me, she lost it all over again. I couldn't take it any longer. I ran over and wrapped my arms around my baby sister.

"Someone tell me what's going on."

At the same time of her demand, Brock's voice came through our earpieces. The duped video feed was running low, and we needed to head out. Reworking the video feed would take too long. John could confirm the men next door were asleep from the laced food. They wouldn't regain consciousness until tomorrow.

Antonio spoke. "We'll tell you everything, but we are running out of time. I need you to get your stuff so we can leave."

"I can't leave. I need to take care of something tomorrow."

"I lost you once. I will not lose you again. Let's get your things packed and get back to the hotel. We'll discuss what happens next when we get there." Antonio was using his authoritative voice on Kat.

Kat stood from the couch and turned her emerald eyes on Antonio. "Do not start with me. I will not put up with your demo—"

Before she could finish yelling, Antonio swooped down and threw Kat over his shoulder. Then he reached down and grabbed his son with his other hand. "Seems my wife has everything she needs. It's time to head out."

Antonio turned and headed for the door. Kat was pounding her fist on his back, demanding he put her down. The cute boy in his arms was giggling at his parents' antics. Those two were perfect for each other.

"I'll grab some clothes for both of them and be out in two minutes." Not waiting for Zane's reply, I headed down the corridor to the bedrooms.

ONCE BACK IN THE HOTEL, tension was high. Kat was still mad about being taken without a choice. Antonio Jr. was watching cartoons on the couch. Antonio seemed to always have an eye on his son.

"Is someone going to tell me what's going on?" Kat demanded.

"Where do you want us to start?"

"The beginning."

Over the next hour, we told Kat where I had been and that I had been trying to get to her. How Sanchez was our uncle, which she already knew. Then how

Sanchez faked Antonio's death and led him to believe she was dead.

By the time the story was done, Kat was sitting on Antonio's lap with his arm wrapped around her waist. In the couple of years I'd known him, this was the most vulnerable I had ever seen the man.

Brock's face came across the computer screen. He was in his war room, surrounded by his team. His fiancée, Jessica, was sitting next to him. Before he could talk, Jessica chimed in. "Did you know that every year, eleven thousand Americans injure themselves while trying out bizarre sexual positions. That is my PSA for the day. Be safe."

Whenever Jessica spit out facts that were basically useless, Brock's face lit up with joy. He enjoyed listening to her.

"I think we have less time than we planned. I was watching the satellite feed on Kat's house. A couple minutes ago, two cars arrived, and approximately six men headed into her house. They must have been tipped off. It won't take them long to figure out where you are."

"Fuck. We need to get you both back to Ft. Lauderdale now." Zane was pacing back and forth in front of the screen, his hands clenched so tight that his knuckles were turning white.

There was no way I was going to jet off to safety

and leave Zane to finish the mission. "I'm not leaving you."

"We need to figure out what Yermushin and Sanchez are up to at the charity event. I wonder if they are planning the trafficking sale at the charity event," Zane asked. "Did you forget what I promised my brother? I need to hold true to my word. If you're with me, I will be worrying about you and not concentrating on the mission. It was hard enough tonight, going on a mission I knew would come out okay. I can't think about going on this one tomorrow with you there."

Kat wrung her hands. "I know what they're planning. That is why I need to stay. I need to stop them tomorrow."

The room went quiet at Kat's words, and everyone's attention was on her. Since we had been back to the hotel, she had been listening to the conversations and not saying much.

"What are they planning Kat? You need to tell me. It's the only way I can help. Then we can move on with our lives." Antonio said.

"They're selling nuclear codes to the North Koreans."

At her words, the room went even quieter. Everyone sat in stunned silence, wondering how the Director of the CIA could be so corrupt.

"Were you helping them?" Antonio asked.

"How dare you accuse me of that? No, and I shouldn't even have to tell you that! Over the years, I've helped Yermushin with contract kills. I didn't kill any one that didn't deserve it. Each time I was given a mission, I researched as much as I could and decided how to proceed. I tapped Yermushin's phone lines a few weeks back and listened to his conversations with Sanchez. They were talking about the exchange. After it was complete, my mission was to take Yermushin out." Kat was vibrating with anger.

Antonio knew he messed up. "I'm sorry, Kitty Kat. Everything is so fucked up right now. I need you to be safe, or I won't be able to do my job. You, Sophie, and Antonio Jr. need to head to the airport tonight. We will stay back and make sure the codes don't get into the wrong hands."

"I'm a contract killer. Don't you think my skills would be useful?"

I couldn't hold back the question anymore. The need to understand why she hadn't killed Yermushin years ago was eating at my insides.

"If you are such a good killer, why didn't you kill Yermushin years ago for killing our parents?"

Kat's face went pale at my words. Antonio's glare was full force.

"He didn't kill our parents. Sanchez took that

group out years ago. He told me he tracked them down."

Was Kat too young to remember the man's face? When I closed my eyes at night, it still haunted me in my dreams. "Sanchez lied. Yermushin is the one that pulled the trigger on Mom."

"I didn't know."

There was no way to fake the devastated look on Kat's face. She had been led down the wrong rabbit hole, too.

"Do you have the recordings, Kat? If you have him on tape, I need them. This is what my brother needs." Zane was right. Zack could use them to take Sanchez down. I also planned on going through my documents when I got home. Something else was not sitting right with me. I think I must have some information he doesn't want me to have, and he is trying to get it back.

"Sorry to break up the lovely meeting," Brock said over the computer, "but you have incoming guests."

All the men in the room reached for their side arms. The air in the room became thick with tension. Not wanting to wait for Brock to give a step-by-step of the incoming, I reached for the laptop in front of Zane and switched Brock off. After a couple of keystrokes, I was in a private browser and had a connection that wasn't traceable.

The hotel never changed the default password on

the camera system. I got the hotel feed on the first try. The spare laptop on the table came alive with Brocks pissed-off face on the screen.

"Not cool, Sophie. I was about to give you guys the feed."

"Already have it, and I'm pulling up the satellites as we speak. We didn't need your ugly mug on the big screen. Zane and Antonio need to see the feed and get us out of here safely."

Zane leaned over my shoulder. His muscular scent was intoxicating. "Can you pull up the schematics of the building?"

Before he could finish asking for the plans, I was into the hotel's primary server. I did a quick search, and the schematics for the building were on display. Antonio and Zane worked on studying the plans while I worked on tracing the incoming.

Two large SUVs pulled up in front of the hotel, and six large men dressed in military gear jumped out.

"Guys, we need to go." I yelled to the room or anyone that would listen.

Zane ran his hand through his hair and pinched the bridge of his nose. "Antonio and John, take Kat, Sophie, and Antonio Jr. down the back stairwell and through here." He pointed to a back alleyway. "I will distract the men at the front stairwell. After you get them to the airport and on the plane, meet me here." He scribbled an address on a sheet of paper.

"No." I wasn't letting him go after six big military men with no backup. Kat was protesting too.

Antonio grabbed his son and walked toward the door. "Kat, so help me, I need you to work with me and get your ass moving. We will make sure the codes are not sold, but first, we need to get out of here alive!"

The amount of danger before us must have made Kat realize it wasn't time to fight with Antonio. She grabbed her things and followed John and Antonio.

But Zane needed to learn. He had given me my sister back, and I would do anything to help protect him now. "Give me the spare gun. I'm coming with you."

He didn't have time to argue with me, and Antonio and John had already left. He was stuck with my help.

Zane grabbed his Glock from his ankle holster and handed it to me.

Grabbing the last of the things, we headed for the stairwell. The stairwell at night was creepy. Every little sound echoed. The thought of six ex-military assassins heading our way made this stairwell even more disturbing.

We made it down two flights before a door below us opened. The heavy stomping of men coming up the stairs was loud.

Zane leaned over the railing and aimed his gun. With a quick pull of the trigger, one man screamed. The men all fired up. Bullets flew everywhere. The sound of their guns echoed through the stairwell, causing my ears to ring. When the shots stopped, we heard the running of boots up the stairs.

The steps were getting closer. Zane motioned for us to exit out the door. We slipped out the door and closed it enough that only a crack was left. When the men were almost even with us, Zane swung the door back open, and three quick shots felled three men. *Four down, two to go.*

The sound of retreating steps had me puzzled. "Why are they heading away?"

Zane creeped to the door open and took another look into the stairwell. "Those are hired thugs. They are not trained killers. Follow closely and stay behind me."

When we reached the first platform with the three men laying on the floor, Zane felt for the first guy's pulse then looked in the man's back pockets.

"Why are we not getting out of here? Can you stop feeling the guy up?"

"I'm looking for his ID to figure out who sent these men." That made sense. I was glad the super spy was thinking. The copper smell of blood was messing with my nose and my ears still rung from the gunfire.

Five minutes later, we made it to the hotel parking garage.

The black Range Rover we picked up Kat in a couple hours ago was only a few parking spots away. The problem was that there was a thug dressed in military gear standing in our way. His shoulder-length hair was greasy. He was twitching so bad that the gun in his hand was shaking. Track marks ran up and down the crackhead's arm.

I gripped my gun and pointed it at the man standing between us and our freedom. Close by, a car backfired, causing the crackhead to pull the trigger. The bullet was heading straight for me. Before I had time to move, Zane threw his body in front of me.

I heard the bullet hit flesh, and a groan escaped Zane's throat.

At the thought of losing the man I might be falling for, I raised the gun and unloaded the clip into the crackhead. I felt no remorse, only the hollow feeling of losing someone else I cared about.

14

ZANE

Seeing the man standing in front us with a gun pointed at Sophie was one of my worst nightmares. This was the reason I hadn't wanted her along. I was so focused on getting Sophie to safety, that one thug had surprised me.

When the unkempt man squeezed his trigger, the only thing I wanted to do was save Sophie. I didn't care what it cost. I leapt in front of her, hoping to take the bullet and save her life. Luckily, the bullet only grazed my arm. A grunt escaped me. No matter how many times I got shot, it never got easier. I was convinced that the older I got, the more the fucking bullets hurt.

At the sound of my grunt, Sophie emptied her clip into the man who shot me. Sophie killed him, and he was one less man to worry about. There had been one other man in the stairwell, and at the sound of the shooting, he came out from the other side of the garage. I didn't give him time to raise his gun. I shifted on the ground and raised my Sig. With one clean shot, a stream of blood ran down his forehead. Headshot. The six men were no longer a threat. I needed to get Sophie to safety before more men came.

"You're alive."

The sound of surprise made me chuckle. How could she think one low-life thug-for-hire would take me out?

"Of course. You ready to head out? Or, do you need to empty another clip in that guy?"

Sophie's face went from confusion to shock.

"I killed someone for real. What am I going to do?"

We didn't have time for her to freak out. "Yes, you killed someone for real. Not sure there is any other way to kill someone. You emptied the clip into him. We need to head out, meet the team at the airport, and get you to safety.

I couldn't help but groan when I went to push myself up. The bullet had grazed my arm, but it would be okay.

"I heard the bullet hit you. Where were you shot? We need to get you to the hospital. And there is another way to kill people. I have killed people electronically many times. It produces way less blood."

Sophie was not only deadly with a gun. That woman was deadly with a computer. There was no way I would go to the hospital, though. Sophie has a one-way plane trip waiting for her.

I unlocked the SUV. "Get in."

I heard the shuffling behind me and knew she was following my orders. Sophie was fuming with anger beside me. I didn't have time to figure out what had her so mad. We needed to get her and Kat to safety.

Once we were on the interstate heading toward the airstrip, I reached into my bag and grabbed a burner phone. Brock answered on the first ring. I clicked the speakerphone button.

"You guys make it out? You left a nice pile of bodies in the stairwell. I've erased the footage of you from the stairwell. The clean-up crew is on its way to take care of the bodies. Did you get any information on the men, or did you just shoot them all and walk away?"

Sophie shifted in her seat. "Brock, we need to get Zane to the hospital, and he's not listening to me. He's shot." I could hear the concern in Sophie's voice.

If Sophie had been shot, I would have headed to the hospital. I understood where she was coming from. But, she was more important than the graze I got from the bullet. Once I knew she was in the air and on her way to safety, I'd have Antonio patch me up. We had to work on our game plan after the women were safe.

"How bad?"

I couldn't help but roll my eyes. "It was a graze. I'll be fine."

Brock understood the importance of getting Sophie and Kat to safety. John was flying back with the women. Brock's team and Asher would escort them from the airport back to Blackwood Security. Kat and Sophie would stay there until Antonio and I killed Yermushin.

"What is the ETA on Antonio?"

I could hear Brock's fingers clicking across a keyboard. Over the short time I'd known Brock, he had impressed me with his skills. I wasn't surprised, since Sam Blackwood had given him Blackwood Security. The last time I had spoken to Sam, he had been dealing with issues in Shialia and didn't have time to give Blackwood the attention it needed. So, he and his future wife gifted the company to Brock. What most people didn't know was that Brock had owned half of the company as a silent partner.

"They are only five minutes ahead of you."

I glanced over at Sophie. She was gazing out the window. Her shoulders were still tight with tension. I wanted to make this a little easier.

"Thanks, Brock. Do Bridget and Jessica know Sophie is coming back to Blackwood today?"

At the mention of her friends, she looked at the screen, waiting for Brock's reply. When he let her know they would be there, it seemed to help with the tension.

The streets were clear in the middle of the night, and we made it to the airfield in no time. I pulled onto the airstrip and noticed the other Range Rover parked next to the Boeing 727. The nice part of this op was that we had so many billionaires' planes at our disposal. The Boeing 727 was Blackwood Security's private jet. The jet had a mission control room built in that most security firms would drool over.

The second the car came to a stop, Sophie jumped out. I had to jog to catch up to her. If she thought this was the end of what we had started, she had another thing coming. The more time I spent with her, the further I was falling for her. I still didn't know if it was lust or love. Either way, we would spend time together to figure it out.

I gently grabbed Sophie's arm to stop her so we could talk before she left.

"Sophie, stop."

She spun around at the sound of my words. "What? You got what you wanted."

Damn, if it wouldn't be harder to break this

woman's outer shell than it was to shoot an apple from two and a half miles away.

"I'm far from getting what I want. I want your body spread across a bed with my tongue between your legs, begging me to make you come."

"Our fling is over. I got my sister. You will take down the director and save the world. It seems like you don't need my help at all."

That was where she was having a problem? She didn't want to be cut out of the op? The problem was that she was a computer hacker, and when she had faced down danger, she drained a complete clip on the target and saved no bullets for the other man coming after us.

Antonio and I needed trained field agents to take down Yermushin before he sold the codes to North Korea. The more time I spent with her, the more I wanted her around. If it weren't nuclear codes being sold, I would be on the plane with her, heading home and coming up with a new plan to take down the director.

"That's why you're upset? You want to come on the op?"

Sophie turned and looked over to where her sister and Antonio were in a heated discussion. At least I wasn't the only one with a pissed-off woman.

Her voice almost came out as a whisper. "I want to

take him down. He stole so much from me. I know I should head back to spend time with a sister I haven't seen in years, but I want to take vengeance and kill him, and not in a one-clip way. I want to tie him up and torture him for years."

Her declaration of wanting to kill the director made my blood rush to my pants. When I shifted to get more comfortable, Sophie noticed, and a knowing smirk came across her face.

"If it was a simple kill mission, I would set you up as a sniper and let you take him out. But we have to deal with Yermushin first and stop him from giving away the codes. I don't think the Director will be there. When we finish this mission, I will make sure you get your vengeance."

At my declaration, Sophie threw her arms around me. "You mean it? You won't kill him or hand him over to your brother on a silver platter?"

It would cause my brother issues if I didn't hand him over. But, I would give Zack enough information to know the Director was dirty and make it look like he fled the country. That way, we could handle the Director the way we wanted for hurting the people whose lives we cared about.

"Yes."

Sophie pressed her soft lips to my mouth. My body hummed with energy. I wanted to lay her down in the middle of the tarmac and have my way with her. I slipped my tongue into her mouth. It was pure pleasure to hear her moan against me. Needing to continue with the mission, I pulled back.

When I broke the kiss, we were both panting, and Sophie's eyes were filled with desire and hunger. I wasn't the only one ready to throw down on the tarmac.

Needing to taste her again, I went in for another kiss, but I was interrupted by coughing.

Not caring if I was holding us up, I pressed in against Sophie, and the kiss was even hotter than the last one.

"Hey, they need to leave!" Antonio shouted.

I pulled back slowly, enjoying the look of need on Sophie's face. "I'll be at Blackwood Security tomorrow night, and we will continue where we left off."

Sophie turned and walked toward the airplane. Her tight-fitting jeans accented her perfect ass, which had a little extra sway. I knew what she was doing, and it was working. Before she made it to the plane, she turned around and reminded me that I had promised not to take him out.

Once Sophie and the rest of them were on the plane, and I saw the wheels leave the airstrip, I let out a breath I hadn't even known I was holding. Brock would phone me the second the plane landed in Ft. Lauderdale and everyone was safely locked away at Blackwood Security.

I wasn't the only one happy they were on their way to safety. When I looked over at Antonio, he seemed to have relaxed a little.

"Ready to go save the world from an attack they have no clue is coming?"

Antonio reached up and scratched his head. "Isn't that what we always do? People live their lives, not realizing how many times they have come close to being wiped out."

15

SOPHIE

The smell of bacon and laughter brought me out of my sleep. The last couple of days floated through my mind, with Zane at the center of all my thoughts. Zane was tantalizing and made me want things I wouldn't ever be able to have. He deserved a woman that could give him the world.

The laughter was getting louder, and I knew it was time to get up and face everyone. I had wanted to stay up and talk with Kat, but it was hard. When we had made it onto the plane, she laid down with Antonio Jr.. He needed his sleep, and we had both been through an emotional roller coaster. The adrenaline was wearing off, and I fell asleep in my chair before the fasten seat belt sign came off.

Mia, one of the operatives that worked for Brock,

woke me up when we landed. I hadn't even woken when the plane hit the airstrip. John had been carrying Kat off the plane, and Asher had had Antonio Jr. in his arms. I should have known he would have been there. Asher was Antonio's twin and would have done everything to protect Antonio's wife and child.

I could hear the pitter-patter of footsteps running down the hall. We were staying in one of the apartments above Blackwood Security. The footsteps stopped outside my door, and two crystal-blue eyes peered over the side of the bed. When I rolled over, Antonio Jr. had the largest grin on his face. "Aunty, are you going to get up soon?"

I loved being called "Aunty." I reached over and pulled him into my arms. The sound of his laughter when I tickled him sounded like angles. My door opened again, and Kat stood there with her hands on her hips. Her long red hair was wet. She was wearing a pair of jean shorts and a white T-shirt. The smile that spread across her face was pure happiness.

"I told you to let your Aunty sleep."

"I did, Mom. I waited for a whole fifteen more minutes."

Kat walked over and grabbed Antonio from my arms. "I meant until she woke up."

"She's up now, Mom."

How could I argue with his logic? "I'm up. Let me take a quick shower, and I'll come out for breakfast."

Kat took the little man out of the room. He was protesting the whole way, saying I didn't need to take a shower.

The shower felt amazing and helped me wake up. When I made it out to the kitchen, the apartment was full of people. It brought tears to my eyes, realizing the support team I had behind me and the friends I had made the past few years. I caught sight of Brock out of the corner of my eye. I wanted to ask him if had talked to Zane and how the mission was going.

Brock must have been able to tell I was struggling with asking about Zane because he volunteered the information without my needing to ask.

"They made it to the safe house last night. Antonio patched Zane up. We sent out another team to assist them this morning."

I needed to stop thinking about the man. Maybe I would if I spent today going over the data I had compiled over the years and tried to figure out what had triggered Sanchez to blow his cover.

"Brock, can I use one of the stations in your office today." If I were working next to Brock, I would be able to hear any updates about the case and find out anything I needed.

Brock looked like he was struggling with the answer. "Don't you want to spend the day with Kat?"

The guilt rushed over me. Putting revenge to the side is hard. I wanted to take Sanchez down. I was being selfish, wanting to work instead of spending time with Kat. At the sound of her name, Kat joined the conversation.

She propped herself up on the kitchen counter. "Antonio's parents are coming over to spend time with Antonio Jr. I can help Sophie go through her data while they are watching him."

Leave it to my sister to come up with a good plan. I had a feeling she also wanted to know what was happening with the mission. As it was, we would be told only what they wanted us to know. If we were in the room when transmissions came through, they wouldn't be able to keep the information from us.

Brock didn't answer right away. He reached for the spatula and flipped a Mickey-Mouse-shaped pancake he was working on. "Stay out of the mission. If you find something that will help, I will take it under an advisement. Otherwise, you need to stay out of the mission going on."

Kat and I both nodded, but when I looked into her eyes, I could tell she was thinking the same thing I was. We would do whatever we had to in order to protect our men. *Wow, where did that come from?* I was already calling Zane my man. I had never believed in love at first sight. That was something that happened in fairy tales, not real life.

Jessica, Brock's fiancé, walked into the kitchen. "I'm so excited to spend the day in the lair." Jessica seemed to think she was joining us. I took a second to register the shirt she was wearing. It said, "Future Hacker In Progress." I jumped out of the chair and gave her a hug.

"When did you tell everyone?" I couldn't believe they were having a baby. The thought sent a jealous twinge through my gut. I hurriedly hid my emotions.

Brock pulled her into his arms and kissed the top of her head. She was glowing.

"This is how we are telling people. If they see the shirt, they figure it out. You were the first one to notice. I spent the morning downstairs, talking with Mia and the team members still around. For a bunch of operatives, they aren't very observant."

Brock chuckled at her. Everyone had gathered around the counter to congratulate the happy couple on their announcement.

"Have you called Patty and Sam yet?" Patty was Jessica's twin sister and the next queen of Shialia. Since their dad had gone MIA, Patty had temporarily taken over. She would be so happy to find out her sister was pregnant.

Jessica's face lit up with joy at the sound of her sister's name. "Yes, we called them last night. I wanted Patty to be the first person I told, besides Brock. She is so excited. They also set a date for the wedding. It will be in May, which is close to my due date. I will be a whale for the wedding."

"You will be beautiful because you will be carrying my baby." Everyone oohed and ahhed at Brock's statement.

I LOVED BROCK'S LAIR. It was every hacker's dream. He had two stations with eight monitors. At his station, he had three of his screens linked to different missions. On the center screen were Zane and Antonio. They had their heads down, studying the schematics of the building they were going to tonight.

The man could take my breath away. It should be illegal to look that sexy. It almost seemed like he could sense me watching him. His head rose, and when he saw me on the screen, a cocky grin came across his face, like he knew I was checking him out.

At Zane's movement, Antonio looked up, and his eyes lit with joy when he saw Kat standing next to me. "How did you sleep last night, Kitty Kat?" Antonio's deep voice boomed into the office.

A red blush came across Kat's face. I didn't need to know what was going on between those two. Antonio let out a chuckle.

"Fine."

"Where's our boy?"

I had a feeling both men would not be happy with Kat and I digging into Sanchez. *Too bad.* We were both out for vengeance, and it would be ours.

"He's with your parents. Sophie and I will spend a couple hours comparing the data we compiled."

When I saw Zane open his mouth, I held up my hand for him to stop. "Us comparing data will not affect your case. Let us do something. We'll stay in this compound and not leave." I was almost sure we wouldn't leave, but that would depend on what we had found.

After breakfast, Kat and I had sat down to talk about our lives. Sanchez had taken Kat in and informed her he was her only living relative. He took care of her and sent her to military school, where she excelled in becoming a sniper. She was one of the most sought-after snipers in the world. Ice was her special ops code name. Ice was so much cooler than the normal color names the CIA gave out. Kat was also skilled in close hand-to-hand combat. Brock was in awe when he heard who she was.

Sanchez had tasked her with a mission to protect

Yermushin at the charity event. She was supposed to be his bodyguard and make sure the sale went through. When everything was complete, she was to kill Yermushin.

He had promised her this was the last mission. She wanted to retire and work as a social worker. She wanted to have a safe life for her son and not go on deadly missions anymore. The older Antonio Jr. got, the harder it was to sneak off without him asking questions.

Zane pinched the bridge of his nose. I could tell he was holding back. "Go over your data together. Let me know what you find, but you have to promise to stay in Brock's custody until we get back."

"Sure." Did that count since I had my fingers crossed behind my back? If we found something, I would go after the director myself. Nobody would stop me from my end game, certainly not some man I've known less than a week, even if that man made me wish for things I knew I couldn't have.

Kat and I had worked on figuring out our trust. With Kat's knowledge of the director, it didn't take long to find the trust documents. She knew who his lawyer was and the firewall was impressive on the firm's computers. So, instead of spending hours trying to find an open port, I spammed the company, hoping someone would give me their user name and password.

Five minutes later, someone clicked on the spam email and entered the information I needed. People needed to take a closer look at emails before clicking links. In an instant, it worked, and I was in. A couple of keystrokes later, I had the trust information pulled up and copied over so I could figure out how to cut Sanchez out of the money.

The money was funneled monthly into two accounts, one in my name and one in Kat's name. Sanchez would drain the money out of both at the beginning of the month. Kat and I could change the information so Sanchez wouldn't be able to get in anymore. He had set up the accounts when we were kids. Since we were adults, according to the trust, he shouldn't have access to the trust money anymore. With a few key strokes, we cut off his cash cow.

I had to take a second look at the trust. I couldn't believe what my eyes were seeing. Each trust had close to a hundred million dollars in it.

16

SOPHIE

Kat and I had sifted through data for two hours straight. Jessica and Brock had left to grab lunch. Zane and Antonio were going over the guest list for the charity event. No matter how hard I tried to stay focused, my eyes kept wandering to the monitor they were on.

"Sophie! I found something!"

I glanced over at Kat's monitor.

"The Prime Minister of Russia is blackmailing Sanchez."

Blackmailing wasn't the reason he brought me in. There had to be more.

"Okay, explain how that affects me?"

"You're not looking." Kat pointed to the bottom of a page.

Holy shit! The Prime Minister of Russia and Sanchez used to work together. Yermushin was the Prime Minister's younger brother.

"Yermushin and the Prime Minister are brothers. Wow."

Kat let out an aggravated huff. "The Prime Minister has all the information about our parents' deaths, and it looks like our grandparents' deaths too."

Based on a transaction sheet Kat had found, Sanchez was paying the Prime Minister money each month. She was right. Two weeks prior, an email had come from Russia, demanding more money. Sanchez couldn't pay, so he was helping Yermushin sell the nuke codes to North Korea. If he produced the codes, and the sale went through, his debt would be cleared.

"Sanchez must've thought I'd read the email between him and the Prime Minister."

When I stopped returning his calls, he must've thought I was working on collecting data. Then, when I didn't turn over the communication I had, Sanchez must have been worried I would bring him down.

He was smart to have kept my sister and me apart. In one day, we had stopped his money train and figured out why he was after me. What we needed to do was get information from the servers that confirmed he killed our family. That, along with the recording Kat had about the nuke codes, would put the director away for a long time.

"Do the boys have a trace on Sanchez?" Kat was peering over to Brock's station.

We were told to stay out of the current mission, not the mission of destroying Sanchez. Swiveling in the chair to Brock's station, I pulled up the closed browsers. Brock was tracing Sanchez's movement. He was near the meatpacking district. Since losing Kat, maybe Sanchez planned on taking Yermushin out himself.

"You keep digging on the server. I'll look around on the dark web. Sanchez is in New York."

The dark web was a place where you needed to know what you were looking for. Google didn't exist on the dark web. The government had put up false pages, hoping to catch people doing the wrong thing. I was looking for archived data of when a hit might've been placed on my parents. I pulled up a page I was familiar with AlphaBay. AlphaBay was one of the top sites used for hits.

I accessed a well-known hit list page. What I saw made my heart drop. Antonio and Zane were both on the list.

I clicked the link to see who took out the hit, but I didn't have time to look further. I heard footsteps coming down the hall. I exited out of the page ten seconds before Brock walked through the door.

"Jessica and Bridget are upstairs with the food. I figured you guys needed a break," he said.

No, he wanted us out of the room so he could talk with the guys with us not around. I wanted to get Kat's opinion on the information I'd found, so when I saw Kat start to protest, I shook my head at her.

I COULDN'T HELP but smile at the women around the table. Jessica and Bridget each had a container of Chinese food. Two more containers waited for Kat and me to dig in. No matter how much I wanted to have a fun lunch with my friends and sister, Kat and I needed to discuss the information I found online and whether we would let Brock know or be stupid and try to save them ourselves.

"Hey, I need to talk to Kat about something. We'll grab our food and go."

When Bridget's family went on the run for her father's mistakes, they had moved into the same neighborhood CJ and I lived in. Our love for computers made the friendship effortless. The three of us had spent hours together, coding and fine-tuning our craft. When Bridget's previous life came out last year, it hurt that she hadn't told me. I contemplated coming clean about my past, but she had just gotten pregnant. I knew she would want to help, and I couldn't put her in danger.

Bridget smiled and pointed to the chair. "Come on. Don't cut us out. I want to help. Jessica counts numbers all day. We know she needs something fun in her life."

Jessica swatted at Bridget. "My man keeps me entertained." A slow blush crept over her face.

Bridget reached over and grasped my hand. "Tell me what the plan is. How much money do you need, and where are we going?"

"We figured out why Sanchez is after me." I shook my head when Bridget went to jump in. "Kat and I wanted to dig deeper. I was checking out the dark web and pulled up AlphaBay. I wanted to look at the archives. I never made it past the new posting page. Someone hired a hit on Antonio and Zane."

Kat gasped. She leaped from her chair and was heading for the door, but we needed to talk for a second and work this out our way. "Kat, sit back down."

"I'm going after my husband."

"Already planning on it, but we can't walk out of here without someone knowing. Let's formulate a plan, steal a jet, and save these men."

The owner of AlphaBay was an acquaintance. The first step was to get the hit taken down for a few hours. The next was getting back to New York.

"Fine."

"Bridget, can you watch Antonio Jr. while we go to New York? We need guns and plans for protecting them. I also need to borrow Alex's jet somehow.

Jessica nodded immediately. "Alex might ask questions. Royal Airlines has spare planes for us at the hanger. I can call my pilot. Royal Airlines won't say anything to Brock, either."

Words couldn't express my gratitude. It meant so much to have friends that could help at a moment's notice. "Okay, guns. Anyone know how to find them?"

"Sophie, we'll stop by my storage unit in New York. There is only one gun I will use to take this man out," Kat said, propping her chin on her hand on the table.

"Who are you planning on shooting?" I asked. "We'll make sure our men make it back alive. Guns are only needed if someone is in trouble."

Bridget and Jessica both agreed. This was a backup mission, not a search and destroy.

"I've been in the spy game for years. Sanchez took out the hit. I will bet my rifle that he also told Yermushin they were coming for him. Our men will be walking into an ambush."

I reached for the laptop to pull up the schematics of the building. Kat reached over and closed the lid on my fingers.

"What are you doing? We need to figure out everything about the event."

An evil smile spread across Kat's lips. "Nope. Antonio and Zane are planning on taking Yermushin down before the charity event at his warehouse in the meatpacking district. If we leave soon, we can set up in the rafters and wait for the meeting to go down."

Zane would be angry with me for putting myself in danger. He gave me the one thing I wanted in the world. Kat and I would have their backs during the meeting. I was still worried about Kat going on a kill mission, but I knew she wanted to protect her husband.

Kat had broken down and cried this morning after breakfast when we talked about Yermushin. She felt stupid for working with the man that killed our parents. Her need for vengeance was clouding her judgment. The right thing would be to let Brock know what we found.

"Are you sure about this? We couldn't hear anything they were saying." Brock had put the feed into his ear when talking with the guys. He was definitely keeping us out.

Kat shrugged her shoulders. "Yes. When they talked to Brock, I read their lips."

How do you respond to that? From a young age, Sanchez had shaped her into a super spy. Zane and Antonio should have used her on this mission. Kat talked about how Sanchez started taking her to Camp Peary at the age of ten. Camp Peary is the CIA training facility for covert spies. What other super skills would she pull out?

Bridget gasped. "Holy shit. You read lips? When are you going to give a training lesson? These prissy moms at the jungle gym are always catty. I want to know what they say when they are on the other side of the playground. Alex confiscated all of my listening devices."

There were so many things wrong with Bridget's statement. Surprisingly, none of them shocked me. I didn't care about learning to read lips. I was hoping she would teach me to shoot so that the next time I had to kill someone for real and not electronically, I could do it without unloading the full clip.

"Our biggest challenge will be getting out of this building without being caught," Kat said. "This place is covered with cameras."

Reaching into my pocket, I pulled out my phone. It rang twice.

"Hey, Sophie."

"Hi, Daisy. Can you help me? You will get in trouble from Neal."

Daisy was Neal's submissive. She had been kidnapped and tortured for years. She was still recovering and lived with Neal. Neal was Patty and Jessica's best friend, and he ran Patty's security company. There had been talk about merging Patty's and Bridget's companies.

"Oh, yes. Neal has been lax on Daisy. Daisy needs a good punishment." Daisy was a borderline masochist.

It was hard not to laugh when Daisy spoke in the third person. "I need a ride. We will meet you at Chubby's Diner in thirty minutes?"

They wouldn't think to track Daisy's car until it was the last one. Now, we needed to get to the cameras. The only person watching the cameras was Brock. Jessica could help us with our next op.

"Jessica..." It was hard to ask her to get in a fight with Brock. When he found out, he would be angry with her.

"No problem. I will seduce Brock. Let's get you ladies in the air. I called my pilot. He is at the airstrip, ready for you."

When I stood up, Bridget engulfed me in a hug. "Be safe."

Before Kat knew what was happening, Bridget had her arms wrapped around my sister. "Take care of her. I'm trusting you with my best friend."

Ten minutes later, we were slipping out the back

door. I couldn't help but hold my breath for a few seconds, waiting for someone to run after us. No one came. We made it out. *Now, to save the men we love.* I wasn't sure where that thought had come from. We were saving my brother-in-law and someone who helped get my sister back.

17

ZANE

I took a deep breath. Our plan was working out perfectly. We had received intel earlier that Sanchez put a hit out on us. We were working on two cases at once. Sophie might be mad about us killing the director and Yermushin.

Earlier in the day, we were able to get bugs into the house Yermushin was staying at while he was in New York. Antonio's company had some of the coolest gadgets. I thought the CIA gave me amazing technology to work with, but it didn't compare to what Antonio had. We took a drone shaped like a fly with listening and camera tech and flew it into Yermushin's hideout.

We heard Sanchez give Yermushin a list of the codes on a thumb drive. The codes wouldn't work without the key digit. Sanchez was delivering the key digit in person. He did give Yermushin all the information needed to do the sale. He doesn't trust Yermushin not to cut him out. Whoever Yermushin kept talking to on the phone wanted Sanchez killed the second the key was given. And, he was supposed to take out the North Korea operatives coming for the codes.

This was Yermushin's plan all along—to keep the codes for himself or whoever was on the other side of the phone line. They were expecting us tonight. We would walk in and get captured.

Antonio and I taped wires to our body to get the conversation inside the warehouse on tape. We would let ourselves get taken. Once we had the information we needed, Mia and John would take out the targets.

"Ready to get hit a few times?"

Antonio grinned. "It's been so long since someone captured me."

I shrugged my shoulders. "Is it really being captured when we walk in?"

"Good point. Let's go have some fun." I reached to my ear and tested the com back to Mia and John. Everything was set.

Once this mission was over, I would be on the next flight to Ft. Lauderdale to get my woman back. Antonio and I headed toward the meat-packing warehouse. I could hear voices echoing through the open space.

We didn't make it past the front door, before a gun was shoved into my back. Antonio was dealing with the same thing. Our plan was working.

"Who are you?" The man's voice was rough with a Russian accent.

"We came to talk to Yermushin. I think we have information he would want to hear." I held up a thumb drive with the recorded conversation of Sanchez telling Kat to kill Yermushin once the deal was done.

The Russian thugs argued with each other before deciding to take us back to Yermushin. The front of the warehouse was a meat-packaging plant. When we entered the back area, it was full of crates. Each crate was overflowing with illegal guns.

Sanchez and Yermushin were in the center, standing toe-to-toe, arguing. They would get into an even more heated conversation when we gave him the recording. The goal was for them to take each other out. At the sound of footsteps, Sanchez and Yermushin looked our direction.

"Hey, boss. We found them trying to sneak in."

The thug hadn't said we'd tried walking through the front door. If we hadn't wanted to be found, we wouldn't have been. Sanchez eyes rounded in surprise. Interesting. He hadn't expected us to show up.

Yermushin turned toward Sanchez. "Is this your doing?" He pointed in our direction.

Sanchez shook his head. His Italian shoes were tapping on the floor. He was trying to figure out what we were doing. Yermushin motioned for his men to tie us up. We were strapped to two old chairs.

Yermushin was in his late sixties. He had on a black velvet tracksuit with a gold chain hanging down the front. His words were difficult to understand with his thick accent.

"Who sent you?"

When neither of us answered right away, a fist flew in from the side and knocked my head back. Damn, that hurt. I leaned to the side and spit the blood on the floor. Antonio received a punch to the stomach, causing him to lean forward with a grunt.

Like being shot, I thought getting punched hurt more the older I got. When I was younger, I had spent a week in ISIS torture chambers before escaping. One punch from this guy, and my brain was rattling.

"Damn, you don't have any patience. We brought you something in exchange for removing the hit on us."

Yermushin cocked his head to the side. "How do you know I placed the hit?"

I motioned my head toward the director. "I know he told you we would kill you for the codes. I know he told you who we were. And I know you were worried about your men getting caught killing the president's brother, so you farmed out the job."

"This is all interesting information. What makes you think I would remove the hit?"

"Take the thumb drive from my front pocket."

Sanchez was reaching for his sidearm.

"Watch out," Antonio yelled.

Yermushin's men turned their guns on Sanchez.

"I was reaching into my pocket."

It was a lie. Yermushin could tell he was lying and motioned for his men to keep their weapons trained on Sanchez.

Yermushin plugged the thumb drive into the laptop. The director's voice came through the speakers. At the sound of his own voice, the director paled.

"You weren't going to give me the key." Yermushin was reaching for his gun. "We were going to make millions."

The statement was untrue. Yermushin was planning on killing Sanchez as soon as he had what he needed. Both men were planning on double-crossing each other.

"I would give you the key." Sanchez pointed in our direction. "They made that tape up. It's not true. We would sell the nuke codes to North Korea and each go our separate ways. If I killed you, I'd never get out from under your brother's finger."

We had the information we wanted. John and Mia were getting into place. They would take the targets out.

Yermushin gestured to his men. "Kill them, then we will deal with Sanchez."

"Hey man, we gave you what you needed."

An evil Russian villain laugh escaped Yermushin's mouth. "You are no more use to me. Kill them."

The Russian in the red tracksuit leveled his gun. Antonio threw his body at the Russian, causing him to aim down and shoot me in the leg. Fuck, it hurt. But not as bad as hearing the scream of the woman I cared about.

My heart dropped.

SOPHIE

"Why aren't you taking the shot?"

Kat had grabbed a bag full of rifles from a storage unit in Manhattan. I was blown away when we walked into the unit. One wall was lined with guns. The other wall was lined with grenade launchers. I never realized how many grenade launchers existed.

She piled enough guns in her bag to go to war. We arrived at the warehouse before anyone else and Kat had set up her mini kill station.

My stomach had dropped when I saw the two Russian thugs with guns pointed at the backs of Antonio and Zane. When the thug in the red tracksuit arched back and hit Zane in the face, I couldn't take it any longer. If these men didn't die this night, I would work on destroying their lives electronically.

Kat shifted and leaned on her other knee. "Antonio and Zane are planning something. Hold on."

We had all the evidence we needed. Yermushin and Sanchez deserved to die, and I wanted their blood painted on the warehouse floor.

Yermushin screamed for his men to kill Antonio and Zane. When I saw the bullet heading for Zane, I couldn't hold back the scream of anguish. The second it left my mouth, I knew I had made a mistake. Three guns were pointed at us. Zane's lips were turned down, and his jaw ticked in frustration.

Kat didn't even wait for the men to fully turn. With a double tap of the trigger, she took down Yermushin and the man in the red tracksuit. The second thug hid behind a crate. Sanchez ducked behind a stack of boxes.

John came around the corner and, with a quick pull of the trigger, took the last thug out. The only person left was Sanchez. He was hiding in the warehouse.

I needed to be close to Zane. I stood and ran toward the man I had feelings for.

Mia was working on loosening his ropes. Kat and Zane screamed at the same time for me to stop. I didn't listen. I continued, needing to get to Zane and make sure he was okay.

A large hand wrapped around my waist. I could feel the cool metal through my light shirt. It took only a second before Sanchez's cologne hit my nose.

"Everyone back," he demanded.

Sanchez used me as a shield to get to the exit. When he got close, Zane leaped forward. Sanchez moved his gun and fired.

Zane dropped to his knees. Sanchez shoved me forward and ran out the door. Everyone was focused on Zane. They didn't go after Sanchez.

I ran to Zane's body lying on the floor. Antonio was working on ripping his shirt open, revealing a bulletproof vest. At the site of the vest, I relaxed.

John was on the phone with 911, getting an ambulance.

I grabbed Zane's hand and his eyes fluttered open. I could see the pain I caused by not listening. He wouldn't have been shot a second time if I hadn't run after him.

"Fuck!" Antonio screamed.

Time stopped. *No, I can't be seeing this. He had a*

bulletproof vest on. Why is there so much blood? Antonio unbuckled the vest. Zane was losing blood from a hole in his stomach.

I reached to cover the hole and hoped the ambulance would make it here in time.

"You can't leave me."

Tears were streaming down my face. Someone was trying to pull me away from Zane. Didn't they understand I was trying to save him? John squatted next to me. "Sophie, you need to let the paramedics do their job."

I hadn't heard them come in or noticed them standing there. I looked up, and a young man was trying to get to Zane's wound. Another paramedic was putting a mask over Zane's mouth.

I released my hold on Zane's wound, and John pulled me into his arms.

"Zane will be fine. He will be angry at you sneaking out of the house. Brock has been going crazy trying to find you and Kat for the last hour." John's words faded out when I heard the paramedics yell.

"I need the panels. We lost his pulse."

18

ZANE

For three days, I'd been in a hospital bed, waiting for Sophie to come see me. She wasn't answering my calls. Brock and Antonio said she was fine. They didn't know why she wasn't talking to me. She asked for an update every time someone came from the hospital.

The pain was still radiating through my body. The events at the warehouse kept coming back full force. When Sanchez had the gun pointed at Sophie's head, I'd lost it. He used his own niece as a shield to get out of the warehouse.

The soft footsteps entering my room had me opening my eyes. I saw Sophie.

Her emerald eyes were sad. "I didn't mean to wake you."

"You didn't. I was thinking." My voice was horse

from the tube they had in my throat during surgery.

"Hi."

I squeezed her hand. "Stop crying, Red. I'm fine. The doctor patched up the hole. I'm as good as new."

At the mention of my gunshot wound, Sophie started to cry harder. "I can't do this."

"Can't do what? We're sitting here talking. Well, I'm lying down."

She gave me a watery smile. "I did this to you. If you hadn't been brought into the case, you wouldn't have almost died."

The shot to the leg was nothing. The shot that clipped my bulletproof vest and traveled upward, hitting my lung, was bad. The doctor said I coded twice on the table. That made me realize I need to live each day to the fullest. Every thought that went through my head was about Sophie. I wanted nothing more than to spend my life with her.

"The Director of the CIA was rogue. Zack would've called me in on the case sooner or later. I'm mad the fucker is in the wind." When the gunfire started, Sanchez had used Sophie as a shield. Nobody was able to get to him in time. Brock traced his steps, but the man escaped the country.

Zack held a press conference denouncing the Director of the CIA. Sanchez was put on the most-wanted list. Every branch of the government was looking for him.

"Why is it so hard for you to take help from others? I wanted to help you, Sophie."

"You have one of the most well-known families in the world. My parents were murdered, and I spend my time hacking. To top it off, the man I thought was helping me was the one that killed my family."

I reached over, ignoring the pain in my chest, to run a finger across Sophie's cheek, wiping the tears away. At my touch, she started to cry harder.

"Will you have dinner with me when I get out of here?"

She looked into my eyes, astonished. "Why?"

Reaching for her hand, I squeezed. "Because we have something special. I told you on the tarmac I wanted more."

"I came today to thank you. You deserve someone that can give you everything." She reached up to wipe the tears away. "I can't do that."

She kept saying she couldn't give me everything. But, I didn't need everything. She was perfect the way she was.

"I only need you. Explain to me what you think I need." I was getting frustrated talking in circles with her.

Sophie jumped from her seat. "I can't have kids.

The bullet that was meant for my mom—I jumped in front of it. It hit my ovaries. They said I will never be able to have kids."

The sob that broke through Sophie was gut-wrenching. I couldn't handle her being so upset.

"Sophie, come here." I pointed to the side of the bed. When she got close, I reached out to pull her closer.

"Kids are a discussion for a long way down the road. If we decide to have them, we can adopt."

Sophie needed someone to protect her and let her know she was enough.

SOPHIE

It hurt too bad to talk about. Having the choice of having your own kids taken away was hard to deal with. Dr. Roseline, my therapist when I was a kid, said that when I found the right man, he wouldn't care that I couldn't have kids. Her words were echoing through my mind. No matter how many times I heard the words, it didn't change the hurt.

"You say that now, but you don't know." I stepped back, distancing myself from his touch. It was hard to concentrate when he had his hands on me.

The longer I stayed, the harder this goodbye

would be.

"Don't do it," he pleaded.

"What?"

It was easy to say that now. I was falling in love with him. When he wakes up one day and wants his own kid, I will be devastated when he walks out the door. I had lost my family and sister for years. I had revenge to fall back on, then. I didn't have to grieve my family.

It was going to be gut-wrenching to walk away right now. If we spent much more time together, I didn't know if I would ever be able to recover.

"Bye."

"Don't do it, Sophie. Don't walk away from what we have."

What we had would always be in my heart. No one would ever get in there again. I couldn't go through this. "We have nothing."

Anger flashed in Zane's eyes. He pounded his fist on the bed. "That's bullshit, and you know it. Stop running from us."

"I can't do this anymore. Take care, Zane. I'm sorry."

"I will come for you went I get out of here."

A flicker of hope lit deep in my stomach.

"Please don't. It will make it harder for us both. Bye."

The devastation in Zane's eyes was heartbreaking. It would be the last thing I remembered, but he deserved so much more than I could give him.

I turned and walked out the door. Zack was standing on the other side. He looked at me with both anger and disappointment.

It was for the best. I left the hospital in a blur. When I made it to my car, I lost it. I'd just left the only man I'd ever loved.

ZANE

Losing my mom to cancer and watching her wither away in her bed was one of the worst moments in my life. I didn't think I would experience another moment that would come close.

Sophie leaving me was something I didn't think I would ever recover from. Her not being able to have kids was not something I was upset over. I would love to adopt foster kids that needed homes.

I wasn't in the mood for visitors, but the click of dress shoes on the linoleum told me I wouldn't have an option. Had he been standing out there the whole time? Did he hear the woman I fell in love with rip my heart out and leave it on the floor? Maybe she handed it to him on the way out.

If I had known heartache would be this bad, I would have told the doctor to let me code on the table. How can I go on living?

"I'm not in the mood for visitors." I didn't bother looking at the chair Zack occupied. I could see the three secret service agents at the door.

Zack leaned back in the plastic chair. "Will you give up that easily?"

I knew he had heard the conversation I had with Sophie. She didn't want to be with me. She didn't love me as much as I loved her.

"Didn't you hear her? She doesn't want to be with me." The bitterness dripped from my voice.

The man had a country to run. Why was he sitting in my room, talking about my love life? If I wanted advice, I would contact Dr. Phil.

"I heard a scared woman."

Sophie was the bravest woman I'd met. But Zack was right. She was scared to lose the people she loved. She'd had to watch her parents die in front of her at a young age. It took twenty-five years to get her sister back. When Sophie opened her heart, she opened it wide.

I shrugged my shoulders. "I won't go after someone who doesn't want me." It was hard being rejected.

Zack ran his hand through his hair and looked up at the news broadcast. "For someone who has taken on some of the biggest threats to our country and chased people to the end of the world, you are giving up really easily."

"She said not to chase."

"Well, then this will be easier. I need you to come to DC once you are out and help me clean up the rest of the CIA."

That would give me something to focus on. If I spent my time engrossed in work and didn't think about Sophie, I could build a wall around my heart.

"Sure. I'll be on the first plane out."

Antonio stomped into my room. "I told you if you hurt her, I would kill you."

"What you are talking about? I hurt no one."

When Antonio stepped closer to my bed, Zack stood to take guard. I was so pathetic that someone who had bodyguards of his own was trying to protect me.

Zack pointed to the other plastic chair in the room. "Sit down. I put up with a lot, but you won't touch my brother."

"Zack, settle down. I can take on Antonio myself. I don't need you fighting my battles."

Both men grunted.

"When Kat and I were in the parking lot, we saw Sophie bawling. She said she came here to talk to you. What did you say? Kat is trying to calm her down." Antonio was yelling by the time he was done talking.

I shrugged my shoulders. "I asked her on a date. She said we wouldn't work and doesn't want to see me anymore."

Maybe there was hope after all if she was upset.

"That woman looks like she got her heart ripped out."

Zack leaned forward. "Sophie broke up with Zane. She thinks she isn't good enough because she has a medical condition."

"What's wrong with her?"

It was nobody business but Sophie's. I glared at my brother for saying something he had no right to talk about. "It's nothing life threating. She is still my world. The problem is that she doesn't want to be in my world."

"Grow the fuck up and go after your woman. Make her understand that you won't leave her and will always be by her side."

Antonio had a point. I needed to figure out a way to make Sophie believe that, no matter what, I would always be by her side.

"I think you have a good point. I'm not giving up."

Zack stood. "Good. But you need to take care of things in DC first. Then you can fix your love life." Zack exited the room before I had time to respond.

"Your brother's an ass, but the stuff in DC does need to be fixed. I'll watch over Sophie until you get back. Get better, man. You have a battle in front of you."

That I did. I would get her back. It wouldn't be right away, but she would be in my life again.

19

SOPHIE

Three weeks, four days, and six hours. That was how long it had been since I walked out on the love of my life. It was the hardest decision I had ever made. I thought that if I broke it off before it started, it would be easier. But my heart felt like it had been run over by a dump truck.

Nothing seemed to bring me joy. The heartache was so bad that it had caused me to be sick every morning. For the last couple of weeks, I couldn't keep anything down. The smell of coffee made me gag. The only joy I seemed to find was when I held Antonio Jr. in my arms.

I reached for my phone, willing it to the ring, if only to hear his voice for a few seconds. I asked Brock and Antonio how Zane was. I got the same response from them both. They told me to pick up the phone and call him myself. They both seemed mad at me for leaving Zane.

When Kat had shown up at my car in the hospital parking lot, I told her everything. She had said I needed to get over myself and go apologize to the man. Didn't these people understand that I wanted Zane to have everything in life?

Bridget swung my door open and came in, followed by Jessica. Inwardly, I groaned. It looked like both of them were in lecture mode. I wasn't in the mood.

"Looks like she's feeling sorry for herself," Bridget said sarcastically. "If only there was a way to make her feel better."

Every day for the last three weeks, Jessica and Bridget had come into my office to encourage me to contact Zane. The first week, they were sympathetic and listened to me. The second week, they gave me their tamed-down opinions. This week they held nothing back. The filter was gone.

"It's not like he's called me," I snapped.

Jessica played with a plastic bag in her hands. "You left him. Why should he call you?"

Needing a couple seconds to come up with a reply, I clicked the power button on my laptop and waited for it to boot up.

"Have you seen pictures of the man? He's at a

different charity event each night. And, at each event, he has a different woman hanging off his arm. I highly doubt he remembers me."

A week after I left Zane, I had been sitting at home eating ice cream, trying to wash my sorrow away. I flicked on TMZ to see a picture of the man I cared about flash across the screen. He had a woman on his arm. He looked a lot better than I did.

Bridget leaned forward and rested her elbows on the desk. "You really think he moved on, or is he running a mission?"

"Doesn't matter. We're done."

Jessica threw the bag in her hand at me. "No, you're not. Go take that."

I opened the bag. Inside was a pregnancy test. How could my two trusted friends be so cruel as to throw this at me? They both knew I couldn't have kids.

"Is this some sick joke?" I couldn't hold the tears at bay.

Bridget got up, rounded the desk, and threw her arms around me. "No. You said the doctor said you *more than likely* wouldn't have kids. There is a slim chance you could."

It was true. At my last checkup, I had asked what the chances were of getting pregnant, and he said, with the damage I suffered, around five percent. But I still didn't understand what giving me a test and talking about it meant.

"So, I have a five percent chance of pregnancy. Why are you giving me a test?"

Bridget turned to Jessica. "She can't be serious right. Everyone knows."

"I guess not everyone," Jessica replied.

"What am I missing?"

Both women turned toward me and said at the same time, "You're pregnant."

"That's not..."

Over the last couple weeks, I had had a hard time keeping anything down. When food wasn't making me vomit, the smell of it gave my stomach a tumble. Could it be possible? My hands went straight to my stomach. The thought of carrying a little Zane put a smile on my face. But what if I got my hopes up and then was crushed because it wasn't true.

No better way to find out than to take a test. I grabbed the bag and headed down the hallway. I could hear the hurried clacking of heels behind me. When I went to close the door, Bridget was trying to force her way in.

"I will tell you when I find out. You stay on that side of the door."

THOSE TWO MINUTES were the longest of my life. A little white stick held my future on it. Could it be possible the man of my dreams had super swimmers? Two lines appeared across the small screen. I was pregnant. I couldn't believe it. I reached into the bag and grabbed another test. I took six tests before it really sank in.

The need to see Zane was overwhelming. Would he take me back, or would he not want anything to do with me because of my actions? I pulled up my phone. There was an afternoon flight to DC. With a couple clicks, I was on my way.

When I opened the door, Jessica and Bridget had smiles across their faces. They both rushed in and gave me a hug.

"I'm heading to DC." For the first time in weeks, a calm set over me.

Jessica cheered. "About time!"

The flight I had booked was in a couple hours. I needed to run home and grab some things before I left.

"I will call you tonight."

Not waiting for an answer, I rushed back to my office, grabbed my things, and headed for the door.

By the time I reached my car, apprehension began setting in. What if he'd moved on?

I got into my car. As soon as I sat, I heard an audible click, followed by a ticking sound. *This can't be happening! I just found out the best news of my life, and now I'm gonna die.*

Reaching for my phone. I dialed the one person I wanted to say goodbye to. The line picked up after one ring.

"Sophie." His velvety voice came across the speakers in the car.

I couldn't hold in the sob. It broke free. "I'm sorry."

"Red, stop crying. We can work everything out."

He was in DC. If I hadn't pushed him away, he would have been here, and I would have gotten to kiss him goodbye. Instead, I was going to blow up in a fucking car.

"No, it won't work." I heard a growl come from the line. "They put a bomb in my car, and it is ticking."

A stream of cuss words blasted across the phone line. "Where are you?"

"At work." The ticking was wearing on my nerves. I couldn't see a countdown anywhere, I just heard a steady ticking noise.

"I'm on my way. Let me call Brock and Antonio. We will be there shortly. Hold on!"

DC was a few hours away by plane. He wouldn't make in time. "If I don't make it, I'm sorry, Zane. I love you."

"You will make it, Red. I love you. Hold on. I will call you right back."

The phone went silent. I was left with my thoughts about how I had pushed away from the man I loved. Losing my baby would be devastating.

ZANE

It had been hard to be away from Sophie for the past three weeks. Antonio gave me a report each day about how she was depressed and sick. But I promised my brother I would help find the rogue agents.

For the past three weeks, I had been going to charity events and working the halls of Langley to take down all the dirty politicians and agents. The women I'd taken as dates were trusted agents helping me with my case. As of yesterday, we had the information we needed to take down the last dirty politician on the list.

We could never clean up Washington completely. But, we had made a large dent. After the arrests were made, I jumped on the first flight to Ft. Lauderdale. When I landed, I wanted to knock on Sophie's door and demand she listen. But, it had been three o'clock in the morning, and Antonio's words about her being sick ran through my head.

I had planned to surprise her at home the next evening. I had sweet-talked her landlord into letting me in. At first, Betty was suspicious. But when I told her my plan, she gave me access. I was going to cook Sophie a romantic dinner and demand we be together.

I had been baking a caramel cake when my phone vibrated in my pocket. At the sight of Sophie's name on my phone, hope filtered through my mind.

Hope turned to dread when Sophie mentioned the ticking noise coming from her seat. Brock had a bomb expert on his team. John was known for being able to dismantle anything. Ft. Lauderdale police called on him from time to time to help when they were dealing with bombs, and he taught classes on explosives for the FBI and CIA.

I clicked Brock's name in my contact list, and he answered immediately.

"How's the cooking going?"

Over the past few days, Brock and I had been talking. He had been helping me come up with a plan for winning Sophie back. The woman would have to learn that I loved her no matter what.

"Sophie called. She got in her car, sat down, heard a click, and now something is ticking. I need you to send John there right away."

A long pause on the other side had me thinking the phone was disconnected. "John is out of the country on assignment. I'll meet you there. We can FaceTime him, and he can walk us through this."

I made it to White Hat Security's parking lot in

record time. I could see Sophie in her black sports car. She was talking to herself, and tears were streaming down her face. When her eyes landed on me, there was a look of shock.

"Hey, Red." When I leaned in to kiss her forehead, I could hear the ticking noise coming from inside the car.

"You came." She tried to smile through her watery tears.

Needing to see what we were dealing with, I squatted down to see under Sophie's seat. A timing device was attached to enough C-4 to blow up the parking lot. The timer was counting down, and we didn't have much time left. It had hit the five-minute mark.

The running footsteps behind me were an indicator that Brock and Antonio had made it.

"How long?" Brock demanded.

Getting up so Brock could take a look, I said, "Five minutes."

Sophie gasped. "You all need to leave. Get everyone out of here"

No one would leave her to deal with a bomb strapped to her seat. Brock was pointing his phone under the seat so John could take a look.

"It's hard to see without being there. From what I can see, you need to cut the green and purple wires carefully. Twist them together, and then cut the blue. When you cut the green wire, the countdown will go down quick. You don't have much time, so you need to be fast."

Brock reached for his cutters.

"No," I said. "You both have wives and kids. Let me do this. Go make sure everyone is far away in case I fail."

Both men protested, but ultimately left. We didn't have time to debate.

Needing to touch her one more time before I jeopardized both of our lives, I leaned on the door frame. Her lips were inches away from mine. It was intoxicating being so close.

We were still for a moment, then I wrapped my hand around the back of her neck and leaned down. She leaned forward to meet me partway.

I couldn't hold back the moan that escaped my lips. She tasted so sweet. I leaned in, needing more. The ticking of the bomb brought me back. When I pulled away, Sophie whined at the loss of our connection.

"I love you, Red." Not waiting for a reply, I ducked down to work on the bomb.

I ground my teeth as I slowly raised the cutters to the wire. It was now or never. I took a deep breath and cut the purple and green wires. The time rapidly decreased. My hands were shaking so bad that it was hard to get the two wires to connect. Once the purple and green wires were connected, I cut the blue wire. Nothing stopped. The timer was still going.

"How's it going down there?"

"Peachy."

Thirty seconds left, and two wires. One might send us to our death, and one might save us. Orange or red? Those were my choices. I didn't have time to call John back. Red reminded me of the woman sitting in the car, so I reached up and clipped the red wire.

20

SOPHIE

At the sound of the last snip, I held my breath. The ticking should've have stopped. It continued.

"How it is going down there?"

It was a stupid question to ask. Nothing else came to mind.

Zane's reply was a quick snap. "Peachy." His voice was strained.

The shakiness of his response didn't leave me feeling comfortable about us getting out of this alive. I heard the clipping of the wire cutters again. I held my breath, waiting for the explosion. The clicking stopped and it was quiet.

Zane was still crouched down beside the car. I could hear him release the breath he had been holding.

He hadn't had much faith he could disarm the bomb, from the sound of his relief.

"Can I get out?"

I reached over to unbuckle my seatbelt, wanting to get as far away from my car as possible. I never wanted to see the thing again. From this moment on, I pledged to ride a bike for the rest of my life. It only rained in Florida around three o'clock. If I planned my days right, I would be fine riding a bike.

"No."

What does he mean by "no?" I want to get the fuck out of the car. Does that mean there is another bomb?

"I don't understand. The ticking stopped."

Zane looked me in the eyes and ran his hand through his hair. He had a sheen of sweat running down the side of his face. "There could be a second trigger. Brock has the Ft. Lauderdale bomb squad on the way. They should be here any second."

I could hear the sirens in the distance. They were getting closer. When they pulled into the parking lot, it caused a commotion, and people stopped to stare. The SWAT team that showed up had Bomb Squad printed on the side of the truck. Didn't these people understand the danger they were in? Why weren't they running for their lives?

A man dressed from head to toe in body armor showed up next to the car.

"I need you to step away from the car, sir." His voice came out sounding like Darth Vader.

Zane took two steps back. He gave the armored man enough room to look at the bomb and do his job.

When the bomb guy reached for his kit, he noticed Zane was still standing close by.

"Sir, you need to get back."

"I'm not moving. Just do your job, dude. When Sophie is safe, I will move." Zane's jaw was locked tight. There was no room for argument.

When the guy went to protest again, I put a stop to the nonsense. "Bomb dude, that is the most stubborn man around. He's not going to leave. Can we get this bomb removed so I can get out?"

"Dave."

"Sorry, what was that."

This man needed to do his job and stop chit-chatting. I'm glad he wasn't around while the bomb was ticking down. He sure was taking his sweet time disarming the fucker from the bottom of my seat.

"My name is Dave. Not Bomb Dude or Dude. It's Dave."

"Okay, Dave, can we get a move on? I want to get out."

He pulled out a mirror and, for the next five minutes, poked around my seat. When he rose and whispered to Zane, I knew it wasn't good.

"Bomb's under my seat, not his. Time to tell me what is going on."

When Dave turned to face me, his eyes held sympathy. "There is another trigger. To deactivate the trigger, I'm going to have to reactivate the bomb and short the other circuit."

Zane had walked over and was having a conversation with Antonio and Brock. They both looked upset by the information.

"How about option two? You pull me out of here as fast as you can?"

He shook his head. "Won't work. I think I can do this."

No fucking way. What person trying to save your life says, "I think I can do this?" No, you say, "I can do this," and hope you don't blow yourself up along the way.

"Really? You *think* you can do this? You need to work on your bomb-side manners. Repeat after me. 'I can disarm this bomb with no issues.'"

"Red, I will be right here the whole time." Zane had come back while I was giving the bomb tech a pep talk on talking to people trapped with bombs.

If I made it out of this stupid bomb predicament, I would spend the rest of my life making it up to Zane for walking out on him when he was in the hospital.

"No. Please go, seriously. Just go."

"Not going to happen. This bomb expert will finish disarming the bomb, and then I will pull you into my arms, take you home, and make love to you all night long."

"I can't stand thinking that, if this goes off, I will lose you."

It was too much. A sob escaped me. I looked at Dave, hoping he would agree with me. "Please make him leave. I don't want him to die."

Dave disappeared below my seat. For a brief second, the ticking started all over again. Zane was still here. The ticking was counting down the seconds of my life. And then everything stopped. I finally let out a breath I didn't know I was holding.

When Dave backed away with a smile on his face, Zane rushed in and pulled me from the car. He leaned in, and I met him halfway. When his lips crushed mine, the world faded away. The only person who mattered was the man who had his arms wrapped around me. When Zane pulled back and released my lips, we were both panting.

"Zane?"

"Yes, Red?"

"I love you."

"I know."

I slapped his chest. The man was too arrogant for his own good. "Aren't you going to say it back?"

"You're my little red firecracker and will have to wait to find out."

I settled into the leather seats of Zane's Range Rover. I was glad to see him again. My heart picked up at the thought of the kiss. I shouldn't have waited three weeks to contact him. I didn't understand why he was already in Ft. Lauderdale. Was he working a job down here?

We had defused the bomb, but who set it? We still hadn't tracked down Sanchez. He would be the only person left wanting to take me out. Kat and I had made it so that he lost everything. Over the past few weeks, we had worked to track down all of his bank accounts and drain the money. The government was on the search for him.

"I'm moving in with you."

Zane's words threw me for a loop. "You can't demand to live with me. You can ask, and I can decide."

"Clearly, you can't. You need to have someone at your side until we find Sanchez and take him down. You aren't safe alone."

My excitement at his words fell. I was giving him a hard time for demanding, not asking. He didn't really want to move in with me. He was doing it to protect me. Then he would be on his way again, and me and my little peanut would be left to figure out our life alone.

Zane hit his hands against the steering wheel. "You took my words wrong. I want to live with you. I can't think about you not being safe. After we find Sanchez, I want to continue living with you, if you want."

We made it back to the house in record time. I was still pondering Zane's words about wanting to live with me. I knew in my heart it was the right thing to do. But I was having a difficult time with the reality.

Zane was at my door before I had time to unbuckle my seat belt. When the door opened, he pulled me into his arms.

"I can walk."

"Stop fighting me for once. I almost lost you today. I need you in my arms. Please let me have this."

I leaned my head forward and gave him a kiss on the lips. When we walked into Betty's apartment to let her know we were back, she was rocking in her chair with a grin on her lips. When the door to my apartment opened, I was stunned.

Rose petals lined the floor. Unlit candles lined every shelf in the house. The kitchen looked like a flour bomb had exploded. Here was the answer to my question earlier today—what had Zane been doing in Ft. Lauderdale? He had come for me before I called.

The tears leaked from my eyes. I couldn't hold them back.

"What's wrong."

"You did this for me?"

A blush crept across Zane's face. "I had planned to cook dinner and have the kitchen cleaned before you came back, but when you called, I stopped everything and came to you."

I cried harder. No one had ever done anything like this for me before.

"I'm sorry." His voice sounded like I had taken away his new gun.

"You don't understand. I love it. Take me to bed."

"But you're crying."

I stretched forward and placed a kiss on his cheek. "Happy tears. Now, are you going to take me to bed?"

Zane didn't need to be asked twice. He headed down the hallway in three giant strides. My bedroom seemed so small with his presence in it.

The next thing I knew, I was flying through the air. My back hit the bed with a couple of bounces. The hunger in Zane's eyes was mesmerizing. He crawled up the bed and wrapped his fingers in my hair, pulling my mouth to his.

He swiped his tongue across my lips, demanding entry. The kiss was full of passion and need. He deepened the kiss, taking my breath away. When Zane pulled back, a whimper left my mouth. I peeled my eyes open to find his blue eyes swimming with emotion.

ZANE

Easing away from Sophie's mouth was a struggle. When the whimper left her lips, I wanted to continue. The need to be inside her was overwhelming. I wanted to possess her to prove she needed me as much as I needed her in my life.

I worked at pulling Sophie's shirt up her body. Her perfect breast and nipples called to me. While I got her bra off, my mouth was watering to taste her skin. I lowered my head and captured her nipple in my mouth. Her whimpers made me suck harder.

I licked my way over to her other breast. When my lips touched her nipple, she arched off the bed, encouraging me to continue. Needing to taste her everywhere, I worked my way down her body, loosening her jeans and pulling them off her body.

I couldn't hold back a groan when I noticed she didn't have underwear on. She was dripping with need. I spread her legs open and slowly licked her.

"Beautiful. So, beautiful," I murmured against the inside of her thigh. When I looked up, Sophie's head was thrown back. Her back was arched in pure bliss. Moans of passion were escaping her mouth. Her eyes were tightly closed. "Open your eyes. I want you to watch me lick this sweet pussy."

Her eyes flew open, and I could see the need to come was pressing on her. I leaned in and sucked on her clit, working two fingers in and out of her velvety folds. She lost it and came. It was the most beautiful thing, watching the woman I love get lost in the passion.

I couldn't hold back any longer. I needed to be inside Sophie. Throwing my pants to the side, I worked my way up her body, stopping to suck on her round, perk nipples. I could listen to the sounds pouring out her mouth for days.

"Please."

Running my fingers through her hair, I pulled her to my mouth for a kiss. With a thrust, I was buried inside of her. I could feel her folds clenching against me. The feeling was so intense that I had to stop and wait for a moment.

"Move. I need you to move." Her words came out in moans.

I slowly worked myself in and out. I wanted this feeling to last forever. Sophie met each of my thrusts with intensity. I couldn't hold on much longer.

"Come with me now." At my demand, her body let

loose and squeezed me. The feeling of her milking my cock made me lose it. With the last thrust, I was buried inside her.

We were both out of breath. I could feel her heart beating against my chest. I slowly worked myself out. At the loss of our connection, she whimpered.

Needing to take care of Sophie, I ran to the bathroom and got a wet rag. Her face blushed when I went to clean her.

"I can do that," she whispered.

"Don't be embarrassed. I spent a half hour down here, licking you. Why is it embarrassing that I want to take care of you?"

When I was done, I reached up and pulled her into my arms. "See, if I lived with you, I could do that every day."

Sophie was quiet for a while. She bit her bottom lip. "In about eight months, things will change though."

I didn't understand what would happen in eight months. "What are you talking about? Are you going to let me move in?"

"Yes, and in eight months, we will have our baby."

Baby? What? Can it be possible? She had said she couldn't get pregnant. It was all moving so fast. But, I knew the first time I saw Sophie, that she was it. I hoped what she said was true.

"Are you pregnant? You said it wasn't possible."

When Sophie went to shy away, I pulled her farther into my arms.

"The doctor said it was near impossible. I had somewhere around a five-percent chance. Are you mad?"

"No. I'm happy. Tomorrow, we will find a more secure place to live. I will be by your side at all times until Sanchez is found."

When Sophie went to protest, I held my finger up to her lips.

"I love you, Sophie. Let me protect you."

"I love you, too, my super spy."

EPILOGUE - ANTONIO

The bomb placed in Sophie's car was a warning. He was still out there. My family was not safe until he was dead. I didn't care if Zack wanted him brought in alive. He'd messed with my family too many times.

"Dude, you look like you are going to kill someone."

I looked at where the bomb tech was removing the last of the bomb materials from Sophie's car. "I'm dreaming about all the ways I'm going to dismember his body."

Brock grabbed a stick of licorice from his pocket and popped it in his mouth. That man had an addiction. "Whatever you need, let me know. I'm going to take the afternoon and spend it with my family. You should do the same."

The mention of my family brought the sun to the dark day. Kat and I had found a comfortable routine. I still struggled with losing out on so much of my son's life. But getting a second chance to be with my wife and kid meant the world to me.

I pulled my phone from my pocket. A picture of Kat and Antonio Jr. at the park was on display. I couldn't ever get enough of them.

I dialed Kat, and she answered immediately. She had wanted to come down to where Sophie was. It was hard for her to stay back, but it was for the best.

"I want to see her."

I had a feeling it was going to be a few days before she and Zane came up for air. That man had a lot of hunger to work out. The two of them had a lot of issues they needed to work out together.

"Hello, Kitty Kat. I'm sorry to say that Zane has kidnapped your sister. We're not going to see them for a few days."

"About time that man got off his ass." My woman was a deadly spitfire.

I loved her feisty side in bed. When she had her legs wrapped around me, nothing mattered but the woman in front of me.

"You want to meet me for lunch? Afterward, we can break our son out of pre-K jail." Antonio loved his new school. Each night, he would show us all the new things he learned. When he came home with a picture he drew of him and me, it took everything to hold the tears back. The next day, I framed it and put it in my office.

At the rate he kept bringing pictures home, the whole wall at work was going to be covered in his artwork.

"Sure. I'll head out now." Her voice floated across the line.

The Greasy Spoon Diner wasn't far from White Hat Security. Inside, Kat was sitting at Patty and Jessica's normal booth. Over the last few weeks, Kat had been spending a lot of time getting to know the girls. They had taken her in as one of their sisters.

Her red hair was glowing in the beam of sun coming in from outside. I leaned down and gave her a kiss on the forehead.

"Hello, Kitty Kat."

Her smile lit up the room. "Hey."

"How did it go?" she asked. "Do you know who planted the bomb?"

I wasn't one hundred percent sure who set the bomb, but I had a good feeling I knew who it was.

I nodded. "We think it was someone Sanchez hired."

Sophie leaned back in the both. "How? We drained his accounts."

Sophie and Kat might've drained the accounts. Men like Sanchez don't make it as far as they do without doing favors and being owed favors. The bomb was extremely sophisticated. That was how we ruled out the Russians. We thought the Prime Minister might have retaliated for taking out his brother. "We are going to have John take a look at it when he gets back. He will be able to find a signature on the bomb. People might owe Sanchez favors. He's desperate and will do whatever it takes to get his money back."

"It's my fault." Kat laid her head in her hands. "At the warehouse, I hesitated to kill him. He raised me. I know he killed my family, but I was with him for fifteen years. When I hesitated, he got away."

I reached across the table and grabbed her hand. "Kat, look at me. You weren't the only one in that room with a gun. It's was not all on you to take him out."

"What can I get you guys?" the waitress asked. She appeared out of nowhere.

"We will both have the special." I had learned that Kat liked trying new things each time we went to a restaurant and always ended up ordering the special. Today, we were having a fried cheeseburger.

"Got it. Two specials. Anything else?" the waitress asked.

"Two glasses of water, and we should be good."

EPILOGUE - ANTONIO

The waitress nodded before taking our menus and heading to register.

"I promise we will find him." Needing to change the subject to something less dark, I asked, "Did you find a school yet?"

Kat had decided to go back to college and get a degree in psychology. She had been working on applications to all of the colleges.

"University of Central Florida has an online psychology degree program. I applied this morning. I'm hoping to hear back in the next couple months."

My phone was vibrating. I reached in and pulled it out. Antonio's school was calling. I swiped to answer.

"Mr. Ross." I clicked the phone to speaker so Kat could hear why the school was calling.

"This is Mr. and Mrs. Ross."

The lady's voice on the other end was shaky. "We need you and Mrs. Ross to come to the school immediately. Antonio Jr. is missing."

The End

BOOK LIST

White Hat Security Series

Hacker Exposed

Royal Hacker

Misunderstood Hacker

Undercover Hacker

Hacker Revelation 7/31/2018

The Steele Brothers Series

Montana Fortune 6/26/2018

Visit linzibaxter.com for more information and release dates.
Join Linzi Baxter Newsletter at Newsletter

HACKER EXPOSED
WHITE HAT SECURITY, BOOK 1

Bridget carries a lot of guilt over what happened to Alex Ross and his family. She had been good friends with the Ross boys until her greedy father lost part of the Ross family's savings in a pyramid scheme. He went to jail, and Bridget and her family changed their names and went into hiding.

Bridget imagines that Alex and his brothers feel just as betrayed as she does by her father's criminal acts. When she meets Alex again as a young hacker and the owner of a White Hat Security, he has something more important to talk about than her father's transgressions. A million dollars has been stolen from his company, and Alex needs Bridget's help to track down the culprit.

Alex has certainly grown up since they last met.

The man looks like a Greek god, and Bridget can't help but be attracted to him. As she digs deeper into the theft from Ross Enterprises, Bridget doesn't need any more distractions. This is a more dangerous job than either Bridget or Alex expected. The thief is willing to go to incredible lengths to evade the police, and the two amateur sleuths find themselves caught in the crossfire.

ROYAL HACKER
WHITE HAT SECURITY, BOOK 2

Secrets aren't meant to be kept...

Patty and her twin, Jessica, seem like typical modern women, both successful and self-confident. When Patty suspects her brother-in-law is cheating on her sister, she uses her secret hacking skills to track him to a BDSM club. After Patty confronts her brother-in-law at the club, the owner, Sam, seduces her. Several months later, Patty's life is turned upside down when someone dangerous begins stalking her.

But there's an even bigger secret—Patty and her sister are the daughters of the King of Shialia, and Patty is next in line for the throne. Fortunately, Sam is there to protect her, body and soul. And he's going to have to work overtime, because everyone around him has their sights set on Patty. She's worth a lot of money, but Sam is the only one who knows she's priceless. And just when everything seems to work out, fate has a way of turning the tables.

MISUNDERSTOOD HACKER

A life that should have been a dream...

Jessica Beckett is trying to put her life back together. *Again*. She should be used to danger and drama, it came with the royal territory. She might be a Princess, but she's no 'princess'. No, she's tough because she had to be. After living through a kidnapping and cheating husband, Jess is ready for a fresh start. Unfortunately, there are new attempts on her life. And there's only one man she can trust with protecting her body... but can she trust him with her heart?

Became a living nightmare.

Brock McKenzie is a security specialist. But protecting Jessica is becoming more personal every day

—and night—he spends with her. He knows mixing business and pleasure won't end well, but Jessica is more than business. She's pure pleasure, the kind of woman who brings out his Dom personality. But she's got trust issues from a life filled with traitors to the Crown and her royal family. Brock knows Jessica is the woman for him. *If* he can keep her alive from those determined to kill her.

Can he find her before it's too late?

LINZI BAXTER'S VIP CLUB

Sign up for Linzi Baxter's VIP Club for the latest news, giveaways, experts, and more.

It's completely free to sign up, and I will never spam you. It's easy to opt out at any time.

Click here to sign up!

Click here to like Linzi Baxter Facebook Page!

PLEASE LEAVE A REVIEW

If you enjoyed this book, I would appreciate your help so others can enjoy it too. Review it. Please tell other readers why you liked this book by reviewing it on Amazon.com. Thank you!

LINZI BAXTER'S VIP CLUB

Sign up for Linzi Baxter's VIP Club for the latest news, giveaways, experts, and more.

ABOUT THE AUTHOR

Linzi Baxter lives in Orlando, Florida with her husband and lazy basset hound. She started writing when voices inside her head wouldn't stop talking until the story was told. When not at work as an IT Manager, Linzi enjoys writing action-packed romances that will take you to the edge of your seat.

She enjoys engaging her readers with strong, interesting characters that have complex and stimulating stories to tell. If you enjoy a little (or maybe a whole lot) of steam and spice, don't miss checking out White Hat Security series.

When not writing, Linzi enjoys reading, watching college sports (GO UCF Knights), and traveling to Europe. She loves hearing from her readers and can't wait to hear from you!

Made in the USA
Monee, IL
14 January 2020